T0318006

EXPOSURE

Those Who Love to Watch and be Watched
A Mischief Collection of Erotica

Mischief
An imprint of HarperCollins*Publishers*
77–85 Fulham Palace Road,
Hammersmith, London W6 8JB

www.mischiefbooks.com

A Paperback Original 2013

First published in Great Britain in ebook format by
HarperCollins*Publishers* 2012

A catalogue record for this book is
available from the British Library

ISBN-13: 9780007534821

Set in Sabon by FMG using Atomik ePublisher from Easypress

Find out more about HarperCollins and the environment at
www.harpercollins.co.uk/green

CONTENTS

CONTENTS

Issues and Returns
Janine Ashbless

Don't they say, 'It's always the quiet ones you need to watch'? Well, I was a quiet one all my life. With three older brothers, I never had much choice. I wasn't going to be able to cause as much ruckus as them, and there was always someone saying to Mum, 'At least you've got a nice quiet girl now.' So being quiet was what I was good at. That's what I was told.

As I grew up, I was biddable at school too. I was nice little Kelly, always plodding steadily on. But, when I got my first proper job, I discovered that there's such a thing as Too Quiet.

I ended up working in a university library, you see. I thought it'd be right up my street. I like books, and it was a steady predictable job where you weren't expected to be extroverted. A quiet job.

Quiet? It was like being buried alive. All day I'd sit at the ground-floor desk dealing with books being issued and returned. I'd scan them and check the computer record and stamp them out. That was it. There were six of us on shift at the desk but we weren't allowed to chat to each other because we weren't supposed to disturb anyone. Not that there was much to talk about. Nothing ever happened. All the other library workers were women. The middle-aged ones were dully married and the young ones acted and dressed like they were middle-aged. The highlight of my day was morning coffee, because if it was a staff member's birthday she'd bring in packs of biscuits to share round.

Seriously, that *was* the most exciting part of the working day.

The only thing that reassured me I wasn't already dead was watching the students. At least they were worth looking at – well, some of them – and most were only a bit younger than me. I liked the boys in the hockey shirts best: not as burly as the rugby players but cuter, and with rock-hard calves. And, although there were banks of computer terminals and an online catalogue which they were supposed to be able to handle themselves, the ones in the sports shirts were usually a good bet for coming up and asking for help.

There was one other part of the daily routine that

made it bearable, and that was straight after lunch when I reshelved the returned books. I could disappear upstairs among the stacks with my trolley for maybe half an hour. Hey, at least I was walking about instead of sitting behind my terminal. I shelved books under Sociology, Biosciences, Modern American Literature and Spanish. I would snatch a few minutes reading here and there if I came across an interesting title – I'm always curious – but mostly this time mattered because I could stretch my legs and escape from the scrutiny of Ellen, the librarian in charge of Issues and Returns. She had a grey bob and a sour expression, and she thought I needed to buckle down with more dedication instead of watching the clock. She didn't know that, when I was staring blankly into space like that, inside I was screaming with frustration.

You see, I like being quiet. But I like *me* being the quiet in the eye of a hurricane. I found that out the hard way. I like to be surrounded by noise, and life, and – let's face it – by men. Maybe it's because I grew up with clumping, arguing, messy brothers. In the near silence of the library, I just found myself getting more and more uptight. And horny. Oh, I was bitterly horny. I'd sit behind my desk surreptitiously eyeing up the students, my face composed to blank, feeling the heat itching between my legs. I'd frig myself desperately every day in the staff toilet, snatch a silent hurried orgasm, then pat my flushed cheeks with cold water before emerging again.

3

I sometimes wondered if the others guessed what I was up to in there, or sensed the heat on me, but I didn't care enough to stop. Some days the jittery arousal was so intense it bordered on the painful; I swear that if I hadn't blown off sexual steam I would have exploded.

Too much quiet. Like an astronaut dumped into hard vacuum, I could feel the blood boiling in my veins.

Then one Friday I found the book. Well, I didn't so much *find* it as have it shoved under my nose on the Returns desk. I'm not going to say what it was titled, but according to the cover it was a collection of lesbian sadomasochistic fiction. Slightly shocked, and feeling a thrill of curiosity, I stacked it on the trolley to be sorted later. But I managed to steal a look at the number on the spine, and felt a clench of triumph and odd excitement as I realised it was in my shelving area.

You've got to realise I don't have any interest in girls. Or pain, either. But the very idea of this filthy book was so outside the normal bounds of my imagination, so taboo, that I had to know more. So that afternoon when I picked up my trolley I was buzzing with excitement. In the lift, I only dared sneak a quick look to check it was still there: white spine, red lettering with a jagged transgressive font. A punk book with a dangerous attitude, that font said. I squirmed inside. That day, I shot through my rounds as quickly as I could, and ended up on the fifth floor with only that one left. I even took it as far as the correct shelf. Then I cast a furtive glance around me. I was alone.

The fifth floor is always quiet. I was in a blind corridor formed of bookshelves, with only a padded chair against the far wall. There were no windows, and the grey metal shelves made eight-foot walls and the ranks of books soaked up most sound. The faint hum of a fluorescent light was the only thing that came to my ears. I opened the book.

I was lost, at once. This was a whole new world to me, and I was carried away. I didn't understand all of the vocabulary: it was an American book and I didn't know what Crisco was, or a douche, and I could only guess at the weight of meaning in the term 'leatherman'. I was a bit shocked by the hard-edged characters in the stories too, having naively expected that a sub-culture of women would be somehow, well, *nicer* than the norm. Nice? That was a joke. These characters were whipcord-tough, strutting tattooed dykes who played rough. So rough that my cheeks were soon blazing with heat and my eyes wide with shock. I'd never come across the concepts that pain could be necessary to someone's pleasure, that there was power in submission, that sex could be something requiring so much effort and commitment and sacrifice. My mind reeled under the impact of each new image. But I kept reading. Avidly. And as I did I became conscious of a thick wet heat blossoming between my thighs, a tingling ache in my clit, a sensation of opening up and needing to be filled. My hands were sticky on the book's shiny cover. I shifted my hips uncomfortably, over and over. My bra suddenly felt too tight, as if my breasts were swollen, and when I looked down I could see my nipples poking through the soft cotton top I was wearing.

I lifted my hand to my breasts and circled a nipple with my fingertip, finding myself exquisitely sensitised. Even through two layers of cloth I could feel my areola pucker. Experimentally I pinched a nipple, gently at first, then harder.

At that point, my natural wariness resurfaced and I checked around me, but nothing had changed. Satisfied, I turned my attention back to my nipple and tried flicking it this time, hard. The little shock was surprisingly pleasant. But all this was just distracting me from the contents of the book. I settled my gaze back on the page. My hand drifted down and brushed my pubic mound, intending to soothe the itch there. It was then that I finally realised how aroused I was, because once I'd touched myself it was almost unbearable to stop.

Discomforted, I squeezed my legs together. What I really needed was to take the book into a toilet cubicle and finish what it had started, but the restrooms were on the ground floor, their doors in full view of the main desk. What I *ought* to do, I supposed, was shelve the book and get on with my work, since I was already running late. But that was just too frustrating to contemplate. And what, I thought with horror, if someone else took the book out on a three-week loan? Technically, I was entitled to borrow it on my own card, but there was no way I was going to expose my new reading habits to my fellow employees. I stroked my mound again through my skirt, pinching my outer lips gently. It felt so good that I sighed. I checked the exit between the rows of shelves again, for the twentieth time. No one.

I wouldn't take long, I told myself.

I think I was drunk on my new discoveries, high on the glimpse of a freedom from normality, because I wouldn't normally have contemplated getting myself off in a public place like that. But it was easy when it came down to it. I just rested two fingers on my clothed mound, one either side of my clit, and rocked them back and forth while I read. Soon I was sunk in the fiction, more present in the story than in the real world. My clit seemed to burn under the pressure of my fingers. My juices were making a hothouse of my panties and my legs quivered with strain. I didn't have time to wait, I had to do it now, I had to –

I came. My head full of alien dreams, my hand full of pussy, my sex clenching around air. Sliding down the long sweet slope behind the summit, I let out a long gasp and lifted my gaze from the book. And it was then that

I saw the eyes watching me. Not from the exit between the shelves, but through the shelf right in front of me. Dark eyes with darker brows. Masculine eyes. The shelves stood back to back and, through two racks of books, through the gap at the top of a row, somebody standing on the other side was watching me strum off.

I'd no idea how long he'd been there. I flushed brick red, feeling like I was about to burst into flame and leave only a pile of ashes on the carpet.

The eyes narrowed as he smiled. There was a glimpse of brown curls as he tilted his head.

I did what any librarian would do in the circumstances. I rammed the dirty book into its space on the shelf, turned on my heel and pushed my trolley out of there, my head held high and my eyes fixed firmly on the distance, as if nothing had happened. As if I hadn't just been caught fiddling with myself, and my pussy wasn't full of slipperiness and need. I marched straight to the staff lift and rode down to the ground floor with my lips primly pursed. I think by the time I reached my normal workstation I had convinced myself that, if I could just expunge the whole episode from my mind, it wouldn't have happened.

But as I sat at my desk my clit throbbed, wanting more.

Just my luck that that was the day Ellen decided to get on my case. I suppose I'd pushed my luck just that little bit too long, lingering upstairs. She called me in to her office that afternoon and fixed me with her glare. 'Is everything all right, Kelly?'

'Yes. I think so.'

I tried to hide my fear that my playing about had been reported to her, but it wasn't that. Instead, she gave me a lecture on responsibility and good timekeeping, without ever actually accusing me of anything, and I just nodded along to the drone of her voice. In the end, I had to promise to improve my work rate, and she finally let me go.

That night, I lay in bed and feasted on the mental images from that book. As for my voyeur, I'd worked out that the books on the other side of the shelf would have been the Spanish Literature section. Those dark eyes might have been Spanish, I supposed – there were a lot of overseas students on our campus of course, as there were at every university. But remembering how he'd watched me was disturbing in a way that even the most outrageous acts in the book were not, and I shied from the mental picture. It was far too shameful. He'd watched me *come*. And I didn't want to be the object of sordid male attention like that, did I? I mean, I never had. I'd always passed through life unremarked.

I was careful on Monday to be punctual and keep my nose to the grindstone. I didn't even use the bathroom until my lunch break. And I kept my ears and eyes open for every whisper, any strange look that might mean my co-workers had latched on to some gossip about me. But nothing seemed to have changed.

That still left me a choice, when my reshelving shift came round: what was I to do about that BDSM volume? If I was being sensible, I told myself, I should just forget it existed. It was too risky to read it at work and there wasn't any other option short of stealing it. The book was better off dismissed.

But it was preying on my mind. I hadn't even finished that first story, and there were others I was just as desperate to peruse. So, half-cursing myself, I went back to the scene of the crime. I had five minutes, I told myself, and that was all. And before I even laid my hand on the volume I checked through the shelves to make sure there was no one standing on the other side. Which of course there wasn't, and why should there be? What would students know of library routines?

So I started reading again. This time I kept my hands on the book. I finished the story and started the next. And once again I was lost, drawn in over my head, sucked down by the undertow into a realm far from the airy bright world of my own reality. My pulse thumped in my ears like the surge of waves and my skin ran damp with heat. I turned page after page.

A small noise woke me from my private world. I looked up, and there they were: the eyes were back again.

I think I made a little gasp of dismay. He shifted, lifting his head; I saw a nose and lips and a finger pressed against those lips to signify silence and I was too stupefied to react. I just stood there in the grip of my heat, awash with the helplessness of the story's protagonist. I heard a quiet scrape, a sound of books being moved. He was pulling them from the shelf on his side, I realised. One shifted abruptly on the shelf in front of me, at chest height, than fell aside creating a gap. Through the gap emerged a hand. Long tanned fingers. A bare wrist and forearm, the hairs brown but bleached by sun. A little multicoloured bracelet of braided thread, looped twice about the wrist.

'Read,' he whispered.

Obediently I lifted the book again, and fastened my eyes on the page. I didn't protest as he stroked those long fingers down my breast, softly, to the jut of my aching nipple. I sighed, but I didn't pull away. He traced the pert little bump of my nipple and then he plucked softly at it with his fingertips.

I shifted a little closer, following the tug on my tit, right up to the metal shelf so as to make it easier for him. I didn't look. I'd glimpsed mobile, rather full lips, a scattering of immature beard-hair, warm brown eyes. That was sufficient. I wanted to read. I wanted to be quiet. My eyes paced the lines, trying to concentrate on the meaning as he gently tugged down my top to reveal the orb of my cupped breast nestling in its lace. He stroked the skin softly as if petting a small animal. I could hear his breathing, slow and steady. I leaned into the shelf, shivering with pleasure at his touch. While the heroine of the story suffered through agonies, my own flesh responded to his gentler caresses. I only took a deeper breath, momentarily distracted, when he pushed my bra-cup aside and slid his fingers in to heft my breast into the open. He thumbed my nipple, enjoying the play of the engorged point against my soft orb.

Trusting my body to him, I read on. I read while he watched me, tugging and teasing me, with never a word spoken and the only obvious movements those of his hand, though he must have been able to see the pink of my tongue-tip through my parted lips, the flutter of my lids, the glazing of my eyes. Then I heard a whisper and I looked up.

The faintest of murmurs and the turning of his head told me that there was someone on the far side of the stack with him; instinctively I tried to shrink away, but he closed his finger and thumb around my nipple to hold me captive.

'Sshh!' he breathed, as if he were the librarian, not me.

I froze in place, my heart thudding wildly under my disordered bra and tingling breast. There was more scraping of books, lower down this time, and then a second hand appeared through the rows. Broader and paler than the first, it clearly didn't belong to the same man; a red cotton sleeve cuffed with white clasped the strong wrist. Fingers reached slowly towards me at the level of my thighs. With an incongruously delicate touch, they found the junction of my legs through my skirt. Ripples of pleasure shivered through my body as they began to tickle my pubic mound.

'Oh,' I said under my breath. In a strange way it made sense that I should be groped by strangers as I stood feasting on the most intimate fantasies of someone I'd never met. I was boiling with arousal by now, unable to think of anything but the sensations in my flesh and where they were leading. I didn't resist as the lower hand pulled up the soft fabric of my skirt finger by finger and slipped beneath the rucked cloth to explore the gusset of my panties, before pushing it aside to touch me where I was soft and wet and ready and needy. My head spun. I leaned into the shelving, trying to look as if I were engrossed in the book, quivering in every fibre. Fingertips circled my nipple and my clit like they were two halves of a whole. The fires that had been stoked inside me roared hotter. I couldn't turn the pages any more so I just read the same shocking words over and over – until finally I came with a blush and a long stifled moan, surging then sagging against their hands and the shelf.

Quietly they withdrew their arms. I glimpsed dark eyes

13

and that smile once more through the gap. I never saw the other guy at all.

Oh, I was late by the time I got back down to the Issues desk that day. Ellen gave me a look that would have killed wasps. Then she came and stood over me silently as I worked. I had to sweep books over the security plate and slam down the stamp and pretend that she was not standing there, vulture-like, at my shoulder. After ten minutes, she moved away, but I could sense her eyes on me all that afternoon, and every time I glanced towards her desk she would look up and glower.

I was nearly at the end of my shift when two students emerged from the stairs, and I took one idle look at the first and nearly fell out of my seat. It was him: the Eyes. I was certain straight away. Slim, with untidy dark curls, his long fingers crooked around an armful of books, his sleeves rolled back revealing a woven bracelet on his wrist. He was talking to his friend, a broad-shouldered blond wearing a red hockey shirt. The first student's gaze met mine and he stopped talking, and then they both altered course slightly, heading straight for my desk.

I didn't know where to put myself. My mumbled 'Thanks' as Eyes presented his little stack of volumes sounded ridiculous to me and I kept my eyes on the books and the computer screen, though I sure as hell didn't read a word printed on either. My cheeks burned. Only when I pushed the heap back over the desktop to him did I find the courage to look up. His mouth was tightly pursed as if to suppress a smile and his eyes were bright as he dipped his chin in a conspiratorial nod. Hockey Shirt was watching me too, his expression exaggeratedly deadpan.

'Hey.'

'Hi,' I mumbled.

'Everything good?'

'Uh. Yeah ...'

I awaited their mockery. But there was none – only, as they turned away towards the main doors, Hockey Shirt looked back over his shoulder at me and flashed a grin. It wasn't a cruel grin. It just looked cheerful and well pleased.

That evening, I went out and bought lacy new panties and hold-up stockings.

But on Tuesday after lunch Ellen informed me that I wasn't to reshelve upstairs until further notice: she was putting me on to the Short Loan collection for the whole afternoon. That's like a library within the library: the books absolutely vital to course essays are kept there and only allowed out on a four-hour loan. It means that reshelving is a near-constant round and, because it's on the ground floor next to all the staff desks, I couldn't malinger.

The *cow*, I thought.

I was furiously searching for the right place for the *Handbook of Mucosal Immunology* – a book I had no desire at all to open – when a shadow fell over me and there was Eyes, looking unhappy.

'You should be upstairs now, yes?'

I looked around nervously for Ellen, but shelving blocked every horizon. 'I can't. I'm not allowed.'

'Come upstairs.'

'I –' I stopped abruptly. He stood there looking so beautiful, so young and vital. How could I say no to that? 'We could use the staff lift,' I said faintly.

There are two ways out of Short Loans: the turnstile, which is guarded and visible from all the Issues and Returns desks, and the staff lift at the back which needs a security code – but then the security code is the same on every one of the staff doors.

'Come on,' I said, sticking *Mucosal Immunology* into a random gap. I led the way to the lift and we slipped inside. I'm fairly sure no one saw us.

You might think that once we were in the lift together we'd have said something, or touched each other, but I looked at the illuminated numbers and he watched me and we were perfectly silent. I didn't want to ask how his degree course was going or whether he had a girlfriend – of course he would have a girlfriend – or whether he was in the middle of an essay crisis. None of that had anything to do with me. I just wanted my naughty book and his clever fingers and my time out from my life. I was shaking with anticipation.

16

But I got a bit of a shock when we reached our secret alcove among the stacks. There was a murmuring, a furtive shifting, from behind the shelves on either side. And many pairs of eyes watching through the spaces between the books.

It seemed I had a fan club.

'Oh,' I said nervously. But my pussy was suddenly so full and wet that the juices were soaking my panties.

Eyes looked sheepish. 'Read it,' he said as he took the book from the shelf and put it in my hands. 'Just read.'

I was burning. Wet and yet burning. I couldn't think straight. All those young men looking at me? Quiet little Kelly? The thought charged me with extraordinary sensations I'd never felt before.

I put my finger to my lips in a warning gesture all my watchers could see, then went and perched on the leatherette edge of the chair. This was in the days before phone-cameras, you understand, so I wasn't worried about being all over the internet before teatime. I knew how bad I was being but my recklessness only fed my excitement. Eyes stood uncertainly, then started to sidle away.

'No,' I whispered. 'Stay. Watch me.'

So he went to his knees on the floor in front of me, and with a deep intake of breath I managed to lift and open the book. My gaze fell on words of enchantment and terror. Studiously ignoring Eyes – ignoring all of them – I scanned the paragraph, tugging up my skirt with my free hand. Underneath I was wearing sheer hold-ups the colour of smoke, with lacy tops. Not my usual style at all. But this was a special occasion.

I parted my legs.

My panties matched my stockings: dark and delicate and insubstantial. I knew that the tops of my thighs presented two creamy strips of bare and vulnerable flesh between the lace panels; I could only hope the sight lived up to their expectations. I ran my fingers over my mound and between my legs, and found that my pussy was already so swollen that my sex-lips were peeking out around the narrow strip of my gusset. I eased the cloth aside and started to caress the wet slipperiness within.

Honestly, I tried to read. I tried to keep some focus on the page as I stroked my sex and teased my clit. But I wasn't really concentrating on the words, let's face it. It was the awareness of the men watching me that was making me hotter and wetter and more daring with every moment – Eyes kneeling before me, a look of rapt attention on his face and a huge bulge in his pants; and the men hidden behind the books too, staring at my spread snatch, doing who knows what, as they watched me play with my wicked pussy.

But I kept the pretence up. Leaning back, I held on to that book, one-handed, and kept my gaze upon the page as much as humanly possible, while I stroked my glistening pussy until I couldn't keep my hips from writhing and my breath was coming in tight quick gasps. Impatient, then, I hitched my hips and tugged my panties down, stretching them across my thighs.

Eyes leaned in, his pupils so dilated that his eyes looked black. He groped his crotch with one hand. I opened my fingers wide for him, spreading my pussy lips to let him see, and bucked my hips invitingly. His tongue flicked across his teeth.

That was too much for me. My arousal was at such a pitch that I couldn't pretend to be oblivious any more. I reached out and gestured him to me with a frantic clawing motion, and he understood. Catching at my panties, he pulled them down past my knees, parted my thighs and swooped. I felt the heat of his breath as he ducked in and planted his mouth on my open pussy, lapping at the bead of my clit, kissing and sucking and licking at me. Maybe that wrecked the view for everyone else; I was past caring, I was so turned on. And with a man taking care of my pussy I had a hand free to tug down my top and bare my right breast.

My nipple felt swollen and hot as I tugged it. I arched my back, lifting the book with a hand that shook wildly. One last go at reading: I still tried to make sense of the words even as he pulled one of my thighs over his shoulder so that he could get his mouth in good and tight to my sex, so that he could tilt me to the correct angle to delve

19

his tongue right into my wetness and taste that honey. But I certainly can't recall now what I read then; just the incredible sensation of being kissed and sucked and licked into a squirming abandon so absolute that I lost my footing and just surrendered to his mouth, my gasps recklessly loud in the silence and my body arching and my limbs spasming, under the glowering ranks of books and the eyes of my unseen audience.

* * *

I got a new job a few weeks later, working on the enquiry desk at the city tourist office, dealing all day with people needing help and information, looking for timetables and accommodation and directions. I loved it. I was the calm at the heart of the storm.

But for the rest of that term before I left the library, every Friday, I went up to the fifth floor and gave the university hockey team a private show. On the very last day, I even let them take it in turns to kneel before my chair and lick my pussy. They seemed to like that. They stood around me in a circle as I came, over and over again, writhing on the leatherette and spasming with pleasure.

But I made almost no noise. After all, it's a library. You have to keep quiet.

Missus
Sommer Marsden

He scared the shit out of her, popping up over her back fence that way. Gina clutched her chest for a minute and waited for her fluttery heart to settle.

'Dear God,' she said mostly to herself, but he heard. She knew he heard because he shot her an adorable crooked grin that could only be pulled off by youth.

'Sorry, missus. Thought you saw me.'

'No. I didn't.' She wheezed it more than said it and then tried her own smile on again. 'So you're my new neighbour?'

She was deliberately ignoring the way the slow lazily drawled *missus* had suddenly taken root deep in her belly. Causing her face to flush in a way that had nothing to do with the heat and humidity.

'One of them. My parents bought the house. I'm just here until school starts. Junior year of college, here I come. Few more days, though. Rick.' He stuck his hand out over her fence. Big hand, deeply tanned and firm and smooth. He was a kid, really. Of course he was firm and smooth.

'Pardon?'

'Rick. My name? It's Rick.'

Oh my God. She was mental.

'Hi, sorry. Sorry! I told you, you startled me right into stupidity.'

That was a lie. His beauty had *stunned* her into stupidity.

'Gina. Gina Monroe. Nice to meet you, Rick.'

He tipped her a nod, grey-green eyes doing a subtle but noticeable sweep of her. 'Missus,' he said again.

She felt downright naked despite her black shorts and her grey tank top and her flip-flops. The baseball cap on her head seemed to weigh a ton and Gina became overtly aware of her top sticking to her sweaty skin. No bra. How hard were her nipples? Her mind was racing.

She shook her head. 'Um. Where are you from?'

She could distract herself from the fact that a thick tempo had started in her blood and was now thrumming between her legs. Was this what heat stroke felt like?

Stuart had warned her not to garden in the middle of the afternoon. Early or late was his motto. Before ten or

22

after dinner. Never at two, which was roughly what time it was.

She had heat stroke, that was the answer.

'Alabama,' he said, watching her slyly.

She almost said 'What?' because she'd already forgotten her question. But she caught herself and for that she was grateful. 'I can hear it in your voice.'

He nodded. 'And I can hear the city in yours.'

He was eyeing her lazily now. Gina was positive he knew what kind of chaos was going on inside of her and that he'd caused it. She didn't often respond so viscerally to men – *any* men – but certainly not young men. She had nothing to say. Her tongue was stuck to the roof of her mouth and her brain had shut down.

So when his head turned and he said, in that sinful rich drawl of his, 'Cable man's here. Guess I have to go let him in,' she nearly fainted from relief.

'Nice meeting you,' she managed.

'You too, missus.' Then he was gone.

Gina watched him recede like a mirage. Tall and lanky, leanly muscled and deeply tanned – this was a young man who spent a lot of time outside. Broad shoulders were hidden beneath a washed blue T-shirt that was probably soft as sin to touch. Gina imagined herself pressing her cheek to that fabric. Feeling the solid muscle beneath, smelling sun and young man and summer air on him.

'I have heat stroke,' she said to herself.

But it wasn't heat stroke that drove her into the cool of the basement and into the small powder room. Stuart was somewhere in the house puttering around or watching golf. He'd never know.

She locked the door and pushed down her shorts and panties and ripped off her gardening gloves. As she planted her ass, aching from all the squatting while she weeded, on the navy-blue fuzzy toilet-seat cover, her fingers went instinctively to where she needed them. One attacking her swollen throbbing clit with a trembling touch, two more buried deep into her cunt. She narrowed in on her G-spot – so hot, so confused, so very needy she just wanted to get off.

Gina did not need finesse. She needed an orgasm. How long had it been, she wondered, but forgot to care as she hooked her fingers and banged that plump spot deep in her pussy into submission.

Her fingers delivered just the right amount of pressure while visions of a twenty-something young man ricocheted around inside her head. That soft T-shirt, those tanned hands, grey-green eyes and plump kissable lips. The short brown hair that fell just so over his brow and, Jesus God, that honeyed twang saying *missus* ...

Gina came with a hoarse cry that she immediately stifled by biting her lips. Her back slapped the whitewashed wall and she continued to thrust slowly as her pussy flickered with aftershocks. She rolled a lazy fingertip over her clit and enjoyed the sudden and brisk sweetness of the moment. How long had it been since she'd done *that*?

A sharp knock made her jump.

'Yes?'

It had to be Stuart, who else would it be? But it still startled her and for a moment her stunned brain supplied her with a porno-movie vision of the young stud standing on the other side of the door. Knocking. Wanting to come in and milk another sugary orgasm out of her ... his way.

'Are you OK?'

It was Stuart. *Of course it is, you twit!*

'I'm fine. Just finishing up. Why?'

Her voice was high and watery and guilty as hell. But it had been so good. So unexpected and so ... feral. Her hands were shaking and she washed them well to get rid of the earthy scent of her own sex.

'I thought I heard you yell,' he said to the door. When she pulled it open, he stepped back startled for a moment. 'Are you sure you're OK?'

'I am. Why?'

'You're flushed is all.' He put the back of his hand to her cheek as if to prove it.

Gina didn't see it coming. She simply grabbed her unsuspecting husband by his ears and hauled him in for a kiss.

'Gina, are you –?'

'Shut up. Shut up. Have you ever done it in a laundry room before?'

'No,' Stuart sighed as she kissed his neck greedily.

'Take your pants off.'

Stuart didn't take much convincing. Twenty years of marriage had slowed them down a bit but they still got it on regularly and were pretty creative. But nothing like this. Not this hurried heated coupling that usually came only from brand-new connections.

He licked her nipples the way he always did but randomly decided to bite and the bites shot heat right through her middle, making her chest burn and her pussy flex. Gina pushed him away, turned her back and presented herself. Ass high, shorts tangled on one ankle, body slick and ready for him.

'Fuck me.'

'Gi–'

'Do it. Put it in me.'

He looked like a man who'd been tasered but he approached her, cock in hand, and slid the weeping tip of himself to her split. Stuart put the head in – only the head – the pressure almost unbearable to her. Gina grunted, pushed back on him, impaling herself.

When he entered her, they both stilled, groaned. And then her proper kind husband shoved her upper body down on the washing machine and truly gave it to her, at one point thrusting so hard into her wet cunt that only the tips of her toes were touching the floor. The washing machine grunted and wheezed like a third part and, when Gina growled, 'Pinch me,' Stuart groaned and pinched her hard.

His lips were pressed together hard and she knew he was close. Gina's orgasm rocketed towards her, slippery and delicious. She flexed up around him, pushed her pelvis to the cool metal and closed her eyes.

Well-worn cotton, grey-green eyes, sticky-sweet drawl. She came.

Stuart muttered, 'Thank God.' His fingers bit deep into her hips as he drove into her and then he was coming too, letting loose some warrior cry she'd never heard from him before.

When they finally parted, he kissed her, pushing a long stray lock of dark hair behind her ear. 'What got into you?'

She shrugged. *Missus* ... 'Nothing. I guess I just got a bit overheated.'

Stuart smiled. And Gina, she couldn't help grinning like an idiot.

* * *

Stuart was asleep. Snuggled up in their proper bed with their proper white sheets and their dust ruffle. The kinky laundry-room doggie-style sex over but not forgotten. Stuart had been super-attentive all night and Gina had repeatedly found herself flushed, warm and smiling for no reason.

Gina wandered into the guest room with a glass of wine. Her summer robe clutched tight around her middle. Her body pleasantly sore, her mind pleasantly astounded.

Rick from Alabama waiting for school to start ...

It whispered through her mind and Gina sipped her wine and said, 'Has made you a pervert.'

She blinked once, twice, three times, sure that what she was seeing out of the guest-room window was a hallucination. Too much sun, too much lust, too many orgasms – as if there were such a thing – had twisted her mind. But the mirage of a lean handsome young man raised a hand to her and smiled.

In what must be his new room, at least until school started, stood Rick, plainly visible to her across the small expanses of their dark back yards. From her perspective, a doll-sized but perfectly rendered version of himself.

Shirtless.

'Oh, God.'

There were several heartbeats where they simply stared. She wondered what he would do. She also wondered why she hadn't done the sane thing and tossed him a friendly wave and then left the room. Or shut the curtains.

Or anything that would indicate she had sense left in her head.

'Oh, God,' she echoed herself because Rick was unbuttoning his jeans and drawing down the zipper.

His gaze remained pinned to hers. Apparently, he could make her out just by the small lamp that automatically came on when the room grew dark. Gina had never been grateful that her backyard was so small and the houses on their block were so close … until now.

Her pussy flexed wetly, stomach dropping as if she were in free-fall. Gina pressed her thighs together only to discover that it enhanced the feeling instead of quelling it. In his brightly lit room, Rick with the languid drawl pushed his jeans down and took his cock in hand.

Even from the distance, she could tell he was hung. And hung wasn't even a word she'd normally use, but it suited this young man.

'Oh, Lord. Look away, woman.' But she knew she wouldn't so she ignored her own words.

The most sinful part of it all was that gaze of his locked on her. He knew she was there. He knew she was watching. And he *wanted* her to see.

That alone set off another slippery clench deep in her cunt and she tightened those internal muscles even further to make the pleasure last. She did it again, and again, as he stroked his cock and kept his eyes on her.

He was close to the window. So close that she

wondered if he could feel the warmth of the day still trapped in the glass like she could. Gina had taken several steps forward without even realising it.

The better to see you with, my dear ...

A burble of nervous laughter escaped her but she pressed her body, the cool silk robe whispering softly, to the warm windowpane.

He did the same.

His fist slipped up and down his length. She watched him squeeze, manhandling himself way harder than she would ever think to touch a man. He was rough and rude and fast on his erection and his half-smile turned her almost inside out. A small trickle of fluid escaped her and kissed the tops of her thighs. She was going to need to do something about that or she'd never get to sleep.

When she placed her hands on the warm glass, like a dieting woman lusting after a bakery display, to see him better, she saw him smile. He jerked himself a few more times, cupped his balls and came with a groan she could not hear but could see because his head tipped back a bit. His come splashed the window he was so fucking close to the glass, and that made her shiver hotly from head to toe.

He put his hand to the glass, gave her a nod and she imagined she heard him say *missus*. Then he turned from the window and the lights went out.

Gina sank to the guest bed, facing the far wall. She spread her legs, thankful that beneath her nighty she was bare, and plunged her fingers into her slippery sex. She thrust hard, remembering how hard he'd been with himself. Her free hand plucked and rubbed her swollen clit until she had to capture her tongue between her teeth to remain silent. Her orgasm was brilliant white with bits of pink in the darkness of the dim room.

She flopped back on the bed, covering herself with her robe. Rick, he'd done it to her again. Again ...

* * *

It was really hard to focus on weeds when you kept reliving a hot young guy ejaculating on to glass just for your viewing pleasure, this was something Gina was starting to realise. After the third time she pulled a flower instead of a weed, she sat back with a sigh.

'Bad day?'

His voice was all warm sunshine and hay bales. Gina glanced up with a small start, then laughed. 'Oh my gosh. You are like a ninja.'

'I like it. I'll put that on my résumé. Part-time ninja.'

And sex performer ...

'Did you sleep well, missus?'

'I did,' she said. She felt as if her voice was barely audible. He was pressed the fence, watching her. 'You?'

31

'Pretty good. I usually have pre-going-to-school jitters. Junior year is going to be intense. But, hey, you only do college once, right?'

'Right.'

'I usually find something to do before bed to blow off some steam.'

Like masturbate for the neighbours …

She bit her lip to swallow a crazy burst of laughter. He almost grinned at her, just his upper lip curling a touch to show he could pretty much read her mind.

'You have a good day, missus.' The way he said it made her want to climb the fence and cling to him. Kiss him and touch him and let that stubble she could see on his jawline rub against her own skin and burn her.

'You too.'

And then he was gone.

She waited for her heartbeat to stabilise and her vision, which had gone blurry with the adrenaline rush, to clear. Then she dropped her trowel and hurried inside. She paused to wash her hands because Stuart was that kind of person and took the steps two at a time.

'Hey, there you are, I was just finishing up these numbers and then I thought we could –'

'Fuck me,' she blurted, taking her shorts off right there in the dining room that her husband had set up as his work-from-home office.

32

'What?'

'Did I stutter?'

'N-no,' he stuttered. Which almost made her laugh but she was too far gone.

'Get it up. I mean off. Get them off and then get it up,' she barked.

Gina tossed her cut-offs and her hot-pink panties. They landed by the china cabinet. Stuart was busily working his zipper and getting his pants off. He looked turned on and yet terribly scared, too.

She laughed. 'Don't worry I won't hurt you. Unless ...'

Gina dropped to his lap and put her hand over his. She moved their hands in unison up and down the rigid length of his cock. Stuart, confused but on board, sighed into her mouth as she kissed him.

'Unless what?' he asked as she put the tip of him to her soaked cunt and started to lower herself.

'Unless you ask me to, Stu.'

He blinked at her and Gina took that moment to slide herself down on him and start to move. She grasped his shoulders hard and rocked against him.

'Gina, what has gotten into you?'

His lips were on her neck, her collarbone, his fingers pinching her nipples just the way she liked.

'*You* have gotten into me.' She chuckled. 'You and your big hard cock.'

'Dick.'

'I prefer cock,' she said and squeezed him with her inner muscles.

'You always have.' He grinned at her and she rolled her hips from side to side, erasing that smile from his face. It was replaced with a look of astonished desire.

'Fuck me,' she hissed.

And he started to. As she pushed herself down, holding the chair now to manage her exertion, he thrust up, driving himself deep into her. Gina leaned back, the top of the chair in a death grip. Her hips had taken on a rhythm of their own and Stu had lost his manners altogether. He drove up under her and, when she leaned back just a touch more, his mouth found her breath and he bit her. Just enough. Just enough to drive Gina out of her fucking mind.

And she came.

'Christ,' her husband sighed. Now his hands were on her hips, anchoring her and keeping her just where he needed her to be. After driving himself in balls deep and making a noise she'd never heard from him, he came too.

The spasms deep inside of her subsided but pleasant little blips of euphoria were still firing off randomly.

Stuart looked stunned and finally she touched his nose to draw his attention. 'So what were you saying?'

'Um ...' He shook his head, still looking a bit confused.

'You were just finishing up these numbers and then you thought we could ...?'

'Oh! Take a break together.'

She touched his face. She loved him. The thing with young Southern Rick was just an infatuation. This was the real deal. 'Did that count?' She grinned.

'I think it did!'

'Hungry?'

As if on cue, his stomach rumbled. 'Starved.'

'Let's eat.'

They walked to the pizza place, hand in hand. The sun beat down but when the wind blew you could feel the faintest kiss of autumn in the air.

'So why are you all … worked up lately?' He whispered the last part which amused her.

'I saw something that turned me on. That's all.'

'I wouldn't mind if you saw it again then.' He playfully jabbed her with his elbow.

'Me either,' Gina confessed.

* * *

It was like a weird kind of ritual or something. At least that's what it felt like in her belly. Stuart was asleep and she crept through their house clutching her wine. Trying to keep from gulping it, really. In the guest room, she held her breath when she turned the door knob. He wouldn't be there. It was a fluke. When did he leave for school? Probably any day now. He might already be gone …

It all coursed through her head as she entered.

Halfway across the room she saw the illuminated square of his bedroom window. And, when she stepped up close to her windows, she saw him moving around.

'He's just getting ready for bed. He won't –'

But she stopped then because he presented himself in front of the window and waved. He grinned and her heart lurched and her cunt went hot and liquid. By God, he was beautiful.

Again shirtless, she imagined he'd been doing moving-in chores in the August heat all day. That he'd been sweaty and tired and grateful to get into his air-conditioned house and take his shirt off.

Her tongue went dry as he popped the button fly on his jeans and tugged them down.

And there was that cock again. Big, hard, long, in his tan hand as he kept his eyes pinned to her and started to jerk.

'Sweet Jesus. I am mentally deranged,' she whispered. But she watched anyway, an audible soft pop coming from her lips as her mouth sprang open.

Because, for one instant, he took the tip of his member and slid it along the glass. She could see his skin flatten to the window and she shivered despite the perfect temperature in her home.

He froze, his cock in hand, his eyes on her and pointed.

'Me?' she said aloud.

36

He nodded as if he heard her, but most likely he'd simply seen her mouth move. He pointed again and she considered it. Would she? Could she?

It wasn't as if he was going to touch her or even kiss her! It wasn't as if they were going to fuck.

She untied her robe before she could change her mind and tonight she had nothing under it but a pair of panties. She pushed those down, glad that the layout of the street meant that no other neighbours had a clear view of her window or his.

A blessing because you have lost your mind …

But, even as that went through her head, she pinched her nipples. Being on display was an entirely new feeling. There was something both fantastic and raunchy about it – a heady combination.

She pinched and pinched and, when he jerked his erection hard and nodded, she smoothed her hands down over the ridges of her ribs, over the small swell of her belly, over her neatly trimmed mound and then she touched herself.

He grinned, shut his eyes to show bliss and continued to stroke himself, pausing every few moments to press a thumb to the tip of his cock. She pictured the split there, the small drop of fluid that came with arousal. She pictured sucking him into her mouth and rolling her lips and her tongue over the flared smooth tip of his cock.

Gina drove her fingers deep in her cunt, flexing them greedily and pinching her nipple fiercely. The visions of sucking him off were fuelling her fantasy, fuelling her need.

She inched closer to the window and so did he. He was so tan, so gorgeous – a bronze young god. Much like a statue. Or a wet dream.

She thrust her three fingers deep, her hips banging forward so it ground her clit to the palm of her hand. Pleasure blossomed in her womb and her cunt, and she put her head to the window glass for a moment so that he could see that she was overcome.

She looked up to see him grinning as his hand flew with a desperate tempo up and down his shaft. He pressed a hand to the window and continued to work himself. Even from the distance she could see the tension in his jaw and the tightness in his belly and, when she came in a slow wet slide of spasms, she pressed her hand to the warm window and nodded, nodded, nodded to him with the pleasure of her release. She was done for. He'd done her in again.

He waited for her to glance up and then, with a toss of his head, gave in to his own orgasm, again splashing the window with his come, looking gorgeous and primitive in his abandon.

'Wow,' she whispered.

Her body let off small ticks and pops of pleasure as

her body came down off the orgasm high. He smiled at her and waved and then turned from the window.

* * *

Summer was dying, she could see it. She turned over the browned plants that couldn't be saved and buried them in the earth to help fertilise it. Her legs ached from squatting but she felt good. Stuart had been like a new suitor and they were going out to dinner to celebrate their dirty-dirty sex as he called it.

She hummed to herself and nearly sat down on her ass in the mud with surprise when he said, 'Afternoon, missus,' over the fence.

'Rick,' she said with a secret smile. She felt calm around him now. Not bored, just calm. He still made her pulse thump erratically and her body respond in very sensual ways. 'How are you?'

'Pulling out today,' he said. 'School awaits. Just wanted to say bye to my favourite neighbour.'

Her stomach tingled and she fought to ignore it.

'Bye, Rick.' OK, so she felt a bit of sadness in her belly, but she knew it wouldn't last. The fuel for her sexual fire. 'Be safe and have fun.'

'Oh, I will. I'm looking forward to this year.'

'Make the most of it.'

'I always try to make the most of every opportunity.'

The secret meaning in his words was clear to her.

When she looked up at him, those grey-green eyes were amused. 'That's a good character trait.'

Somewhere a car horn beeped and he turned and waved. 'My friend's getting antsy. Have a good rest of your summer, missus.'

He winked at her and she blushed. She blushed!

'And maybe I'll see you at winter break, you know, around.'

Like in the window ...

She almost laughed. Well, hell, she'd forgotten about breaks. And visits. And all that. Her fire wasn't gone after all.

'Maybe you will,' she said and waved as he turned away from the fence.

Winter wasn't really so far off.

Thief
Charlotte Stein

The first time I watch, I don't mean to. It's an accident, like reading a letter that's not intended for you or going down a road you weren't supposed to. I'm going down this road, and, though it's clearly marked *watching your flatmate masturbate*, I don't turn around and walk the other way.

I stay like this instead. Poised in his closet, the laundry mistake still in my hand. Everything in me saying *leave leave leave*, despite one very real and very unavoidable problem.

It's too late, now.

It was too late thirty seconds ago. Too late after ten. The moment I stepped into his closet and searched for a place to put his T-shirt, my time was up. Because,

41

apparently, Drew isn't the sort to wait around for a while before taking all of his clothes off.

He takes them off the minute his bedroom door is shut. And, when I turn around, that's the first thing I see through the slats in the closet door: my cool, collected, unfathomable flatmate Drew, without anything on.

Though, really, I know that's not the right way to put it. *Without anything on* is the manner in which people describe their elderly relatives, just before they help them into the bathtub. It's almost a joke punchline; it's without a hint of anything sexual.

Whereas this thing in front of me – this thing I can see so clearly in spite of the stripes of wood over this bit or that – it's so … *fleshy*. It's so real somehow, as though all the other naked bodies I've seen in my short life were fakes.

This is what a naked body should be like. This thing, with its broad back and its curving thighs. Even the tiniest detail calls to me, on a man like him – the way his collarbone stands out so heavily against the honey-coloured skin, like dinosaur bones beneath the earth. The way his biceps curve outwards almost delicately, when he reaches up to rub some spot on the nape of his neck.

Though maybe delicate is the wrong word. There's nothing *delicate* about him. It's just the way his skin looks there, drawn taut over the thick muscle beneath.

And he's so pale in places like those, too – on the insides of his arms and below the line where his jeans once rode.

Then down, down, to the thing I absolutely should *not* be looking at. The one that didn't really exist for me until right now, as though prior to this I thought of him like a Ken doll. Smooth, and completely featureless between his legs.

Instead of how he actually is.

There's nothing about him that I'd call featureless. I'm not even sure I'd call it smooth either, because I can see the thick ridge around the head of his cock, beneath the skin. I can see the veins that rope his shaft, so obviously more pronounced than they were a second ago.

He's getting hard, I realise, though God knows why. He's just sat there, on the edge of his neat bed, hands sort of loose on his bollard-like knees. He isn't touching himself or flicking through a skin mag or any of the things I seem to associate with male arousal, so it's understandable when fear suddenly grips me.

He knows you're there, this fear whispers. *He knows you're watching, and he likes it.*

Though I have to say this fear sounds a lot more like excitement, when I start sifting through its contents. Something happens in my body – a kind of twanging, ringing sort of thing – and then suddenly my nipples are stiff and pressing against the material of my shirt. My clit is a little thrum, between my legs.

And I'm wet. I'm wet just at the sight of him, and the thought of him doing this on purpose.

Though it gets decidedly worse, when I realise he's watching something.

I hear it first, before I see its backwash on his flawless face. Just the faintest little sound, like maybe he didn't want to go all the way with it. It's bad enough that he's doing this. Doing it at full volume would be a sin, a crime, he can't possibly.

And then I hear it again – the unmistakable sound of a woman gasping in probable faux-pleasure – and I know for sure. He's watching porn of some type, near silent and not what I'd expected. I always thought Drew was the kind of guy who didn't need anything like this, who had girls falling all over him and no desire to spend lonely nights servicing himself.

But I guess I was wrong. He *is* going to service himself and, even stranger than that, this doesn't feel like something he did just by chance. It feels like a ritual, almost. Something he carefully plans and then enacts, which sounds crazy until I see his face.

He's caught, I think. Rapt. Something about the thing he's watching makes him mindless, and, oh, I can relate to that. I feel mindless right now, just stood here taking him all in. I mean, I don't particularly *want* to stare at his now solid and very stiff cock. I'm not proud of that fact in the slightest.

But I'm doing it, anyway.

And I carry on doing it, when he puts one big hand around himself.

Slow, he does it, slow. Deliberate, I think, though I have to say there's something about the move that seems almost ... separate from the rest of him. His real self is somewhere far away but incredibly close, as he works his hand up and down that glorious shaft.

Because it is glorious. Of course it is. The rest of him is so big and heavy. How could his cock not be the same? It's gleaming wetly at the tip, leaking already, even though he's barely done anything at all. And it curves so steeply, so beautifully. Oh, God, I shouldn't be looking at him like this.

I know the difference between the two: staring out of curiosity or mild fascination, and staring in a weird, fetishistic sort of way. This is the latter, and it's disgusting, I know. *I* am disgusting, as I watch my oblivious flatmate masturbate slowly to the most arousing-sounding porn.

But the strangest thing happens as I do. I find I don't care. Not in the slightest. I'm not ashamed, the way any decent person would be. I just want to see him climax all over that big working fist. I want to see him arch up off the bed, eyes closed, body twisting into an almighty orgasm.

And I want to see it quickly, brutally – dear God, I'm almost greedy for it. I don't even have to run a hand over one stiff nipple to spark another wave of arousal, though I'm sorry to say I do it. I rub myself as he rubs himself, pleasure gushing through my now utterly soaked sex, everything in me on edge, for his big finish.

It's coming. I know it is. He's trying to hold it off – to work himself slow and easy, in time with the rising action onscreen – but I can tell he's not going to make it. He twists the palm of his hand over that swollen head and his face creases right down the middle. His teeth bite into his lower lip.

Three feet away from him someone gasps, *oh yeah, spill on my cock*, and the effect gets worse.

He likes this part, I think. It gets him hot to think of a woman coming all over someone's stiff dick. Though more than that he seems to like her almost genuine moans of pleasure, the sounds of her possibly going over as he jerks himself harder and faster.

Soon, I think, *soon*, and then for some unfathomable reason I'm almost stood on tiptoe. I'm leaning towards the door, watching and watching as he groans out his own pleasure. He has one hand clasped in the sheets by his side, and it's the strangest thing.

The sight of that is somehow more arousing than the slick slide of his fingers on his cock. I can see it pushing there, almost levering his body up off the bed, and then quite suddenly it happens.

It's like a dam breaking, or a pressure valve giving, or some other cliché about things letting go, that somehow seems very clear and almost perfect, right here and now. Something inside *me* lets go, as the first thick stripe of come spurts from the tip of his cock, all over his still working fist.

He doesn't even seem to care that he makes a mess. He just does it, spilling copiously on to the carpet, on to his big thighs, into his hand. And he moans loudly while he does it, too – even that one little trace of control lost.

But I can't blame him. It looks incredible, like he's lost in pleasure, and, more than that, like he really doesn't give a shit. For once, careful, composed Drew is not caring about anything but the pleasure coursing through his body, and the slick feel of his own come, and finally the little ebb of sensation at the end that makes him sprawl back over the bed.

That makes him run one lazy hand over his big perfect body in a way that fills me with a strange sort of envy. *I* want to be the one stroking him, touching him, feeling him shudder with its aftershocks. I want to be that hand on him, though of course I can't be.

I'm only watching. I'm a thief. That's what I've done here: I've made myself a thief.

* * *

The second time I watch, I'll be perfectly honest, I *do* mean to. It's not even a question, really. It's just something there, lingering in the corner of me. The desire to watch him again, as he does things I never dreamed he would do.

He's just so stoic, that's the thing. When I see him the next day, after the first time, he's so different to the way he'd seemed in the bedroom. He says good morning to me, for God's sake. He makes polite chit-chat and reads his crisp newspaper.

While underneath there's a guy who masturbates in some strange, almost ritualistic way to filthy pornography.

The two ideas can't match up in my head. Instead, I have to create two hims: one who seems like a pond of still water, and one who takes all his clothes off and sits on the end of the bed to start this thing all over again.

Though I suspect right from the off that it's different this time. In fact, I know it is. For a start, he doesn't start rubbing himself, all slow and easy right away – even though his cock stiffens far quicker than it did a few days ago. And he doesn't let himself linger over the action onscreen either.

He just pushes back on the bed until he's almost sprawled over it, and then reaches for the bottle of oil on the cabinet by the pillow.

Of course, I hold my breath. I can't help it. I've no clue what he needs the oil for, but my head almost automatically floods with a million vague images. Some of them tame. Some of them bizarre – like maybe he's going to spread it all over the sheets and then writhe around in it.

Though it could just be me who wants that last one. In fact, I'm pretty sure all the images in my head are just me, wanting some very specific things. I want to see him gleaming, I think, and all golden in the low light, and I don't really care how unlikely such a fantasy is.

I mean, realistically, guys do not cover themselves in baby oil before they pleasure themselves. He's just going to put a little bit in his palm and then slick his already heavy shaft, to make it all a bit sweeter – and that's OK. That's totally cool. He doesn't have to do anything more than that for me to steal my piece of voyeuristic pleasure.

Though, when he actually does do more than that, I have to admit, I go up on tiptoe again.

I'm just not expecting it, that's the thing. It's so rude, and even more at odds with the person I thought I vaguely knew. The person I vaguely knew is reserved, conservative almost; he certainly doesn't slide an oiled finger between the cheeks of his ass, and stroke over something I didn't even think guys liked to acknowledge. Guys don't have holes there. They're smooth, like the Ken doll I thought he was. There's nothing to rub over, nothing to fondle and certainly nothing to push into.

Though I suspect he does all three. In fact, I can see him doing all three. After a moment, his head goes back against the pillow, and those long, long legs of his spread in the lewdest way possible, and then he just eases two fingers into his ass.

Just like that. Like it's nothing.

I swear to God, it's so far from nothing. My heart is rattling around inside my chest, and for the first time I really consider echoing some of the things he's doing. I mean, I'm not sure I could actually touch myself where he's touching himself. But then, it's not like he's just doing that alone.

He's also stroking his cock, as he fucks himself with those two slick fingers.

I could do the first part, right? I could stroke my clit, as he does this frantic and extremely lewd thing on his bed. It's getting almost impossible to resist, because I'll be perfectly frank: I've never seen a man behave the way he's doing.

And it's electric. It's like watching someone shape-shift into a different creature, right before your eyes. He's groaning far louder than he did before, rocking against those pumping fingers in his completely stretched open hole. His hips are jerking up to meet the hand he's got around his cock, all rough and jerky; it's like nothing I've ever imagined, even in my most lurid fantasies.

But it's also far more compelling than any of that stuff. My hand has crept to my own breast, without my permission. I'm almost pressed to the slats, so greedy for more suddenly, so desperate to see what it looks like when a man fucks himself like this. When he comes from the feel of a finger stroking over his prostate and a hand rubbing roughly over the head of his cock.

Though, when it happens, it's something of a disappointment. Not because it isn't glorious – because it is. He grunts so loudly and so forcibly it's like he's trying to expel a demon out of his own body, and the long slick ribbons of come spurt out hard enough to touch the underside of his chin. And it's not as though I'm short-changed in the length department, either, because the whole thing seems to go on forever. He works and works and works those fingers inside himself, eking out every last drop of pleasure from his orgasm.

It's amazing. Only, once it's done, it's done. That's it. My weekly moment of something wicked is over, and I have to do the furtive, silly thing now. I have to sneak out while he's in the bathroom, and bury myself under the covers on my bed.

I have to pretend that I don't like this, that it doesn't mean anything, that I'm not a bad, bad person for intruding on someone's most private moment. And, though all of those things have their own little frissons of illicit pleasure, they don't have anything on actually being a part of something.

Even if I'm not really a part of it at all.

* * *

51

The third time isn't just on purpose any more. It's practically a pattern, a routine that we've struck up without his knowing it. I wait inside his closet at a certain time. He comes in and peels off all his clothes.

And then I hold my breath, in anticipation of what he'll do next.

Of course, I'm expecting something big this time. Last time he fucked his own ass until he came all over himself, so it's going to have to be something spectacular. Though, I have to say, when he finally does something …

It goes beyond even my most insane and perverted imaginings. So far beyond that I cover my face with my hands the moment he does it, as though *this* is the thing I can't bear to see. I can't watch this, I can't. Even if he clearly thinks I can.

'You can come out of there now, Susie,' he says, as loud as a gong. As loud as my world ending. He's naked and he's poised on the verge of doing his usual thing, but suddenly I *am* a part of it – real and whole.

And I don't know if I want to be. I'm not sure I *can* be. I'm just not built that way, I'm not prepared for something like this. I thought he hadn't known at all, but clearly he had.

He knew, and yet he did those things all the same.

'Susie,' he says again – so much more forceful than he is usually. Of course it's shameful that this excites me, but I guess I can no more help that than I can help all of the things I did.

I watched. I intruded. I stole. And now it's time to pay the piper.

'You're really not fooling anyone,' he says, at which my face flames red. I mean, I know I'm not fooling anyone. That wasn't my intention – to fool. And yet somehow I'm not leaving the closet.

As though I could just melt into the walls, if I stayed here long enough.

'Come out, and we can talk,' he says.

But I'll be honest. I think he's lying. I don't think he wants to talk at all, and, even if I tried to pretend as much, his nakedness is an awfully big clue.

One that gets bigger, when I finally step out of his closet.

He's hard. Of course he is. If I'm excited, then he's got to be, though I'm not sure why I come to this conclusion. Apart from his thick stiff cock sticking up between his legs, he's as implacable as ever. He watches me with those cool still eyes for what seems like an age, before finally breaking the tense silence.

And, oh, God, he doesn't go with what I think he's going to. No accusations, nothing about what I've done. Just that crisp voice, and a number of words I don't want to hear.

'It's my turn now,' he says.

Of course, I think he means *I'm going to fuck you*. But then he just sort of takes hold of my sides and steers me in front of the television, before sitting back on the bed. Eyes on me at all times, as I stand helpless before him.

'What are you waiting for?' he asks, and I suppose I know then. It's fairly obvious, I think, though I can't quite bring myself to do it without some final say-so from him. He's been dictating this thing all along, so why should it be different now?

Even though it is, it is.

'Take off your skirt. Then I want you to put your hand inside your panties,' he says.

I try not to moan in despair. I know he's serious, but still some part of me hopes it's all just pretend. I dreamed this, I never did any of this, I'm not guilty, your honour.

Though, for someone innocent of all charges, I seem to take to my punishment pretty quickly. Too quickly, I think, as I slide out of the second-to-last barrier between us. And then of course my face heats past red and all the way into some unbearable level. My legs don't want to hold me up; my clit thrums wildly between my legs.

And when I just barely stroke over it – hand struggling within the confines of my underwear – I almost lose every part of myself in the pleasure. I gasp, I shake, I think about saying his name. I think about giving myself over to something for once, and almost do. *Almost*.

'That's it,' he says. 'Touch your wet little pussy.'

And then *almost* becomes *definitely*.

I've never heard him speak like this. In truth, I've hardly heard him speak at all. Once, we had a conversation about a book we both happened to be reading. We've exchanged pleasantries, and shared mundane details about our day.

But never like this. Nothing like this.

'Stroke your clit,' he says, and I almost faint right there on his carpeted floor. It seems like a miracle that I not only manage to take in his words and understand them, but that I also obey him without question.

I slide my finger through my embarrassingly – and loudly – slick folds, searching out that little swollen bud again. And when I really and properly find it, God, when I find it … it doesn't feel like a part of me any more. It feels like some other, secret thing I've uncovered, some new centre of pleasure that shouldn't actually exist.

A burst of thick sensation goes through me, as good as an orgasm but not quite all the way there yet. Despite its intensity, I know there's more to come, but, Lord, I don't know if I can take it.

The sense of which gets worse when he tells me to do other things.

'Do you know what I want you to do now, Susie?' he asks.

No, I think, in reply. *No no no*. Though, in all honesty,

I'm not sure I'm actually answering the question. I'm just shoving a refusal out there, with the mind powers I don't have. *No no no, please don't do this. Please, I can't.*

But he isn't listening.

'I want you to take your panties down, turn around and bend over.'

How is it possible that I'm still standing? I don't even know. And I definitely don't know how I manage to obey him. It seems like an almost monumental effort, one that gets bigger as I wriggle the material clumsily down over my shaking legs.

I turn around and face the television that remains resolutely off, with thoughts of what this means flooding my mind. If I bend over for him, I can never go back. I'll always be this girl who spied, and then took her humiliation. We won't be casual acquaintances any more. We won't share little breakfast anecdotes between mouthfuls of cereal.

We'll just look at each other and *know*.

But I do it anyway. I bend right over, past the point of what he asked for. I don't even crook my knees or do it to the halfway point – I just make a neat fold in the middle of my body, and clasp my ankles, for good measure.

Of course, he can see everything. I think *I* can see everything, and I'm back to front. I'm blind, down here, with just the cool air against every single part of my sex, to tell me what this looks like.

Wet, I think. And so, so exposed. I must seem like some split fruit, all open and juicy and rude, but he doesn't say anything like that. He doesn't make a disapproving sound, and get out his morning newspaper.

He stands up instead, and strokes me ri-i-ight there.

It's not unexpected, but I jerk forward anyway. I stumble, almost, clumsy in this position with my fingers wrapped around my ankles. But that's OK because, even though this is my punishment, he steadies me with those two big hands I promise I never noticed before. He holds me quite still, in the middle of his bedroom, and then just as I'm sinking into a kind of calm he slides the wetness he's gathered up over something he shouldn't.

This time, I don't jerk forward. I sob instead. I think about telling him not to – because I'm sure he would if I did – but the thing is it's tit for tat. I can't say no now, after watching him do what he did.

I have to just stand there and let him stroke over my clenching asshole, with that one unbearably, mortifyingly wet finger.

Though, naturally, he doesn't stop there. He waits until I'm poised on some trembling brink, sure I want to say no but unable to actually express that simple idea, and then he just kind of *presses* against me.

He pushes, he works, he is so diligent in his terrible little task. Oddly, it makes me think of him fixing one of the kitchen drawers – everything about his actions so neat and precise. Dusting things off carefully when he'd done, with just one smoothly running-over-the-wood finger.

And this is the same, in some way, because he isn't rough. It doesn't hurt. He just patiently maps it all out for me, stroking and urging and going about his task so carefully, until that one long finger eases all the way into my wound-up and too tight body.

I don't mind admitting that it's blissful. I really don't. Somehow he's made me do the rudest thing ever, but, as he slides that finger back and forth, I know one thing very clearly. I see it, the way I saw him not so long ago.

This is better than watching. Doing is better than watching. Why steal, when you can have?

'Fuck me,' I tell him, just like that.

And he does, he does. He covers that gorgeous cock of his with rubber, and then he simply slides all the way into the now slick and strangely tingling hole he's only just vacated.

The one I've never actually had penetrated by anything, for reasons I can no longer understand. I can't understand anything, in fact – least of all the person I was, who stood in the closet and didn't do anything about anything. But it's OK, now, because he's filling me up. He's saying things – words he would never have dared to before, like *God I need it, I need this*.

I need you.

Before he wouldn't have said *I'm in need of some salt,*

on my mashed potatoes. Could you possibly pass it over?
He would have just sat there, waiting for something he
didn't think he could just take if he wanted to.

But he can, oh, he can. It feels like nothing I've ever
imagined, to have him sinking so slickly into that tight
little place. To know how excited it's making him, how
jagged it's turning his thrusts, until finally he's panting
and jerking at me just like he did to himself. One hand
scrabbling desperately for my clit, my cunt – *anything*
to make me feel the way he obviously does.

I don't need it, however. I'm already there, buzzing
with every new and strange sensation. The sense of being
filled past the point of bearing, the rudeness of it, the
stroke of his thick cock over every last nerve-ending
around that spread opening ... it's enough on its own.

I'm coming before his fingers have made a full circle
around my clit. I'm coming just from hearing him gasp my
name as though he really knows it, so breathless and exciting
and, ohhhh, God, I can feel him doing it in my ass.

I don't even know what to say about that. Or about
any of this, if I'm honest.

Though I suspect we'll think of something, over breakfast and his daily paper, in the morning.

The Sand Hills Have Eyes
Lisette Ashton

It was automatic to glance around before they settled down for their picnic. Charlotte had been visiting the dunes with Rodney often enough to have an idea of how the afternoon might develop. She cast her gaze over the rise and slope of the surrounding sandy hills, trying to see if there was anything lurking in the scenery's crevices and hiding places.

Trying to see if there was anyone potentially watching.

It was the sort of weather they used to promote the beauty spot in all the best holiday brochures. A hazy sun hung high overhead. The sand was bleached white beneath the heat. The dunes were set perfectly against the Disney blue sky. Even the tufts of marram grass, ordinarily sparse and mangy-looking, seemed to have been shot through a rich verdant filter to make them appear more dynamic and vivid for this afternoon.

The glint of sunlight on something reflective made Charlotte hesitate.

She remembered all those war films she had watched with Rodney where a sharp-eyed marine noticed the glint of sunlight on enemy binoculars. It happened so often in those films she thought it had become something of a cliché. On this occasion, she knew it could just be sunlight flashing from a discarded bottle. Or light catching on some other piece of shiny litter. But she also knew it could be someone watching with binoculars.

Or a camcorder.

The idea made her shiver.

'You OK there?' Rodney asked.

She grinned at him and tried to shrug off the moment's consternation. 'I'm just making sure we're alone,' she explained. 'I think I'm getting a little paranoid in my old age.'

He raised an eyebrow. 'You want us to be alone together?' His tone was rich with faux playfulness. 'What have you got planned for me, Charlie?'

Charlotte fell to the sand beside him and allowed him to embrace her.

They had been seeing one another for the better part of three months now. With the onset of the warm summer weather, they had both been taking advantage of the seclusion of the local sand hills.

Rodney had first suggested taking a picnic there on the weekend. Charlotte had thought the idea quirky and quaint and vaguely old-fashioned. But she agreed. A picnic made her think of wicker cases holding plastic crockery and packed with an Enid Blyton-style feast of scones, cream cakes and lashings of ginger beer. She had pictured boneshaker bicycles and a tartan picnic rug. And, while the picnics did include all those features, it wasn't until they ended up making love beneath an open summer sky that she realised that she and Rodney shared some similar exhibitionist tendencies.

They both enjoyed fucking outdoors.

For her, it was the thrill of sex combined with the danger of potentially being caught in the act. The blend of passion and risk was a cocktail that never failed to set her pulse racing.

But, for Rodney, it seemed he just liked fresh air.

'It's not real exhibitionism,' Rodney insisted during their first time together in the sand hills. 'It's not like we're flaunting ourselves directly in front of someone.'

He said those words when Charlotte was beyond the point of resisting him. His hand had been up her skirt, his sweaty palm resting against the smooth flesh of her hyper-sensitive thigh. His fingers had been teasing in and out of her pussy lips. The squelch of her wetness around him had been as loud as the cries of the overhead gulls. She was eagerly stroking the bulge of his erection through the jersey fabric of his jogging bottoms. He was well built – not the longest she'd ever had but possibly the thickest.

And she tried not to be disheartened by his observation that they weren't flaunting themselves in front of someone else.

The idea of doing just that always melted her inner muscles and made her clitoris throb with greedy need. Anything less seemed somehow pointless.

As she stroked him through the fabric, Rodney murmured words of encouragement for her to do more. She slipped her hand inside his jogging pants, clutched his stiff sweat-sticky length and began to slide her hand back and forth along him.

'Go on,' he muttered. 'That's just what I need.'

And, while Charlotte would have been eager to agree that it was also what she needed, she was beginning to suspect that she really needed something more.

Their relationship had already turned sexual during a DVD night at Rodney's apartment. When they first fucked, his fat cock made her pussy feel full to the point of bursting. He had proved himself a capable and considerate lover and she had been content to explore his fetishes and see if they matched her own foibles.

And, as Charlotte was wanking him on the sand hills

while he fingered her with increasing ferocity, she guessed they shared a common interest in having sex in public places. She changed positions so Rodney could lick her pussy while she sucked more ferociously on his shaft. Because of his thickness, she had figured the extra lubrication of her saliva would enhance the pleasure of intercourse and penetration.

And, while that idea excited her, she was aware that Rodney wasn't really into exhibitionism in the same way that she relished the experience.

The hem of her skirt covered his face. A casual observer, coming across them accidentally, would not be able to see what Rodney was doing to her. Similarly, the fall of her hair discreetly covered her lips as they encircled his shaft.

It was the most discreet form of exhibitionism she could imagine. A diluted version of the raunchy extremes she preferred.

'Do you like doing things in public places, Rodney?' She spoke the words directly to his cock.

When Rodney responded, she could feel the breath of each syllable tickling against her sopping pussy lips.

'I know it's not real exhibitionism,' Rodney insisted. 'Not the hardcore stuff. But I do enjoy having sex outdoors. It seems very healthful.'

She agreed there was a major difference between what they were doing and what others classified as hardcore exhibitionism. If she'd been a hardcore exhibitionist, she would have been posing directly in front of a known audience. She would have been filming herself fucking or masturbating and posting the resultant videos online. She would have been encouraging friends and lovers to film her activities. And then she would have made sure those indiscreet films made it into the public domain.

In comparison to those sorts of antics, what she and Rodney were doing wasn't really exhibitionism. It was simply very discreet and very unimaginative outdoor sex.

They were out of the way in the sand dunes. It was a forgotten beauty spot – desolate and isolated. Rodney always stopped whenever he thought there was a danger of their being discovered: a faraway cough or a seagull screech that sounded vaguely reminiscent of conversation. Charlotte thought it was more like being in the security of a huge private garden, rather than doing anything that ran the risk of their being embarrassed and humiliated for their lascivious indiscretion.

And yet, after that first outdoor encounter in the sand hills, they had returned each weekend to enjoy homemade scones, bottles of pop and a clandestine fumble on Rodney's tartan picnic rug.

This time Charlotte thought his kiss seemed more passionate.

She wasn't sure if there was a genuine increase in his excitement, or if she was simply hoping for the change and transferring her desires on to him.

Rodney's arms were already around her. She could feel the weight of his fingers on the bare skin at the small of her back. As he pulled her closer, his caress slipped inside the waistband of her loose jeans. His fingers trailed over the peach-like mounds of her bare buttocks. And then he was touching the smooth moist flesh of her sex.

Charlotte responded hungrily. Pushing him on to the sand, she straddled him and thrust her chest towards his face. 'Take me properly,' she commanded.

His eyes opened wide.

'Get me naked,' she insisted. 'Fuck me hard. Ride me passionately and make me scream for more so my cries ring out over these damned dunes.'

Rodney cupped her covered breasts in both hands. He grinned warily at her as he massaged the orbs through her clothes. 'I'm not sure either of us would want to do something so bold, would we?'

Charlotte sighed. She didn't *want* to do those things. She *needed* to do them. But she wasn't sure Rodney could see how much she needed to do them. 'Do me properly,' she pleaded. 'Do me with some passion.'

'Properly?'

She leaned back and pulled the T-shirt over her head. The movement meant she could feel the weight of his erection pushing up against her crotch. It was a good solid weight that she knew would be satisfying if not for the barrier of denim separating his cock from her pussy.

Rodney's expression turned to momentary panic when he saw she was undressing. His panic grew more obvious when she reached for the bra's front-fastening clasp and snapped it open. Exposing her bare breasts to him, she felt her nipples stiffen as soon as they were released into the day's warm summer air.

A weight evaporated from her shoulders. The thrill of arousal tingled through her sex. The prospect of being outrageous outdoors was a reminder of so many pleasures she had previously enjoyed before she met Rodney.

His hands went to her breasts.

She wasn't sure if he was trying to cover her, or if he was kneading with the boldness her body craved. Whatever his motive, she thought the result was exciting. She pushed herself into him and then writhed against the bulge of his concealed cock.

'Go on, Rodney,' she encouraged. 'Work me.'

'You're enjoying this today,' he observed.

She giggled and said, 'I love outdoor sex. There's only one thing better.'

He frowned. 'What could possibly be better?'

Charlotte opened her mouth and then closed it again.

The only thing better than outdoor sex was outdoor sex where she knew she was being watched. Nothing could come close to beating that sensation. But she knew she couldn't say as much to Rodney.

She had explained about the limitations of the sand

hills when she had been talking with Darren at the office. Darren was a former lover who was well aware of Charlotte's feelings about exhibitionism. In fact, Darren had been the one who introduced her to outdoor sex and the satisfaction of being watched. He had also introduced her to sex parties.

Not that they went to sex parties to have sex with other couples. Charlotte was always insistent on that point. Charlotte and Darren had only ever gone so that other couples could watch them having sex. In the heady atmosphere of a vibrant sex party, there was a divine thrill to knowing that people were watching as Darren's cock slid in and out of her overstretched sex. There was a giddy appeal to making eye contact with couples while Darren knelt between her spread thighs and greedily lapped at her pussy. It was an experience that added enormously to the pleasure of regular intercourse.

Darren had been the one who urged Charlotte into going commando, so she could 'accidentally' flash any attractive man she saw on the bus. It had only been a small change to the way she dressed. But it had made her constantly feel sexy and special and desirable. It had also meant that, when they wanted to spice up their lunchtime with a passionate fumble in the stationery room, Charlotte didn't have any panties getting in the way.

Darren had also been the one who, on a handful of

memorable occasions, took her dogging. Again, the sex had been strictly monogamous. She had let Darren fuck her in the back seat of his Vauxhall while a crowd of anonymous strangers stared through the windows and watched with wild-eyed desire. It had been a delicious experience. She had seen men masturbating furiously as she sandwiched Darren's cock between her breasts and licked the swollen tips of his glans. She had listened to the audience of masturbators moan with disappointment when Darren insisted that she had no interest in being fucked by anyone other than him.

She had told Darren that their exhibitionism should be governed by a strict look-but-don't-touch policy. And, she supposed, that limitation was what had eventually driven a wedge between them so that she and Darren had to go their separate ways. Darren had wanted to do more at the sex parties than simply be watched. He had been eager for her to do more with the men she excited on the bus and at the dogging sites.

Contrarily, Charlotte was happy to be faithful to him as long as she knew others were watching and getting off on the sight of her getting off. She always said that she didn't need anything from anyone else: except for their undivided attention while she orgasmed.

The separation had been civil and amicable. And, because they continued to work in the same office, Charlotte knew she could always turn to Darren to discuss sex with a confidant who was open and frank and understood her complex drives and desires.

'You're fucking Rodney outdoors?' Darren sounded surprised. 'Rodney from accounts? I didn't think he was an exhibitionist.'

'He's not an exhibitionist. It's not exhibitionism.' Charlotte tried not to sound disappointed. 'We're only having sex on the sand hills.'

'There's not much danger of being seen there,' Darren agreed. 'The sand hills see less people than a blind agoraphobic.'

Defensively, she said, 'There's always the risk someone could be watching.'

Darren laughed. 'Marcia and I went dogging last week,' he explained. 'That was proper exhibitionism.'

Charlotte stiffened so as not to show her hurt. Darren and Marcia seemed to be enjoying the same relationship he had clearly wanted to share with her. There were times when Charlotte wished she could turn back the clock and maybe experiment with some of the sharing ideas that Darren had suggested while they were together. She knew that such 'what if ...?' thinking was never productive or useful, but it was obvious Darren and Marcia were doing all the wonderful things he had wanted to do with her.

'While we were out dogging,' Darren went on, 'Marcia was being watched by a dozen guys. They were all wanking and she picked out the one with the biggest cock. As soon as she had a condom on him, she insisted he took her from behind while she sucked me off.'

Charlotte felt the colour drain from her cheeks. A knot of arousal tightened in her stomach and she dearly wished she could have been with Darren and Marcia at the dogging site, so that she could experience the vicarious entertainment of Marcia taking two cocks. Or maybe participate in the hedonistic spirit of the evening.

'That sounds like more than I would have enjoyed.' The words sounded hollow on her lips.

'I'm not so sure,' Darren said, shaking his head. 'But whether you would have enjoyed that or not is immaterial. I don't think you're enjoying outdoor sex with Rodney at the moment because it's lacking the thing that's most important to you.'

'And what's that?'

He studied her for a moment, his gaze softened with genuine compassion. 'You enjoy being watched, Charlie,' he reminded her. 'Indoors or outdoors – it doesn't matter to you. The only thing that's important is that you have to believe you've got an audience.'

* * *

Now Darren's words echoed through her mind as she kicked off her jeans so she could properly straddle Rodney.

'Charlie,' he gasped. His voice was lowered to an urgent whisper. 'You're naked.'

'All the better for you to fuck me.'

'But –'

He didn't get to complete the sentence. She pushed her mouth over his and basked in the moment. Perhaps Darren was right. Perhaps all she needed was an audience. And, if she could convince herself that there had been a camcorder trained on her before, perhaps that would be enough to make this afternoon's encounter particularly special.

She thrust her chest forward and stood up. The sun bathed her in a warm glow that was reminiscent of a powerful orgasm. 'Kneel between my legs and lick me,' she demanded.

Rodney was pliant and obedient. He placed a hand on each hip and buried his face against her sex.

'Stand up,' she demanded. 'Strip off. Put your cock in my mouth. Then you will take me from behind.'

She didn't know where the barked instructions came from.

She supposed, at the back of her mind, she was trying to give a good show to the imagined audience, the camcorder operator. It was a cheap mental trick. But it seemed it was good enough to get her arousal soaring.

When she knelt on the floor in front of him, fondling his balls and trying to squeeze his thick cock into her mouth, Charlotte was surprised by the liquid heat that surged through her sex. The arousal was total and genuine.

It was only because of Rodney's obvious discomfort that she stopped herself from sucking until he came at the back of her throat. The idea of allowing him to spurt into her mouth would have been wonderful if there had been an audience able to see the trickle of white semen dribbling from her overfull lips.

'Take me from behind,' she urged.

'But someone might ... I mean –'

'Take me from behind.'

There was enough steel in her voice to staunch his arguments. Charlotte turned away from him and fell to her knees. She held her rear up for him like a cat in heat. When his hands fell to her hips, and then guided her towards the tip of his fat cock, she groaned loudly with anticipation.

'Charlie,' Rodney murmured. 'Keep your voice down. Someone might hear.'

She pushed herself on to him. His erection filled her. The thickness was enough to make her feel as though she was bursting. Stretched to her limits, she held back her head and howled with satisfaction.

'I'm serious.' He sounded close to panic. 'If you keep making noises like that, someone is going to hear. They might see what we're doing.'

'Let them hear,' she sighed. 'Let them see what we're doing.'

She thought of saying, '*Let them watch. And, if they feel up to it, let them come over here and participate.*' But she could tell that Rodney was uncomfortable with the threat of their being discovered. And, although she was beginning to suspect that they had different needs, she didn't want to make Rodney feel uncomfortable.

'Ride me,' she pleaded. 'Ride me hard and make me come. Then we can get dressed if that's what you want.'

Obediently, Rodney began to quicken his pace. His length slipped in and out of her sex with piston-like vigour. Her inner muscles were stretched and brutalised by his shaft going back and forth. She reached a hand between her thighs and began to tease the throbbing nub of her clitoris. She knew, when she did climax, she was going to scream loudly, and not because she was trying to upset Rodney.

The cry was rising at the back of her throat because she had bought into the fantasy that they were being watched. Aside from the single camcorder she imagined she had seen before the start of the picnic, Charlotte was also picturing a crowd of enthusiastic supporters urging her on with cries to give him everything she could.

One hand remained pressed against her clitoris, squeezing the bead of flesh with wet wanton fury. The other hand snatched at her breast. She tugged on her own nipple, crushing the sensitive bud of skin and savouring the cruel explosion of pleasurable pain.

'Fuck! Yes!' she gasped. 'Keep riding me, Rodney. Do it faster.'

Her voice had risen to a shrill and demanding screech. She spat each word with enough force to make it roll across the deserted sand hills. When Rodney pushed himself deep into her, and then stiffened, Charlotte howled.

'Charlie,' he exclaimed.

She didn't heed his warning. Her scream of pleasure echoed across the sky. His thick shaft expanded when his climax pulsed into her. She continued crying out as his length throbbed and pulsed and filled her with the scalding heat of his ejaculate.

It was only when the pleasure proved too much that Charlotte finally pulled herself away from him. She curled into a foetal ball and panted softly. Her fingers clawed at the hot white sand. A moment later, when she dared to open her eyes, she was disappointed to see that she and Rodney were alone on the beach. There was no sight of a mysterious man with a camcorder. There were no hordes of appreciative masturbators giving her performance a single-handed salute. Even Rodney had rushed back to the picnic rug to retrieve his clothes.

Darren had been right, she thought bitterly. Outdoor sex alone wasn't enough. She needed to know that someone else was watching her. Without that stimulus, the experience seemed to be lacking a vital ingredient.

75

She turned to glance at Rodney, wondering how she could tell him that this wasn't enough for her. He considered her with a wary expression and she guessed he had already worked out that they didn't have a future together.

Silently, she began to retrieve her discarded clothes.

When she started to walk away from the picnic, he called after her, 'Do you want a lift home?'

She shook her head. 'I think it's best if I make my own way back. Thank you for a lovely picnic. I'll see you on Monday in the office.'

There was a moment's pause and she knew he was working out the subtext to the message: we won't be seeing each other again this weekend – or any other weekend in the future.

And then she walked round the curve of a sand dune and Rodney was behind her and in a past she could no longer see. She continued walking for another half-hour, trudging wearily up steep inclines, and convincing herself that she wasn't lost, before she came to the stretch of road that ran alongside the sand hills.

She recognised a familiar car by the side of the road. A Vauxhall. And, as she walked closer, she saw that the driver was already behind the steering wheel. He held a camcorder in one hand.

'Hi, Charlie,' Darren said easily. 'Fancy seeing you out here today.'

Charlotte glanced into the car. In the passenger seat sat Marcia. Charlotte said a brief hello before studying Darren. 'What are you doing out here?'

'Darren and I have been using the camcorder in the dunes,' Marcia explained. 'It's amazing what you can film some people doing in public places.'

'Amazing,' Darren echoed.

Charlotte studied the couple thoughtfully.

'If you want,' he said carefully, 'you could come back with me and Marcia and watch the footage we've just captured.'

'It's really hot,' Marcia agreed. 'It's this couple and I don't think they had any idea we were filming them.' She paused, then added, 'Now I think about it, the woman looked a lot like you.'

Charlotte smiled. 'And what could we do after we've watched the film?'

Marcia grinned.

Darren said, 'We could do whatever you fancied, Charlie. We've got all weekend. We could upload the film to the internet. The three of us could make another movie. We could do whatever you like.'

She smiled. There were lots of things she liked and Darren knew most of her preferences. The chance to do those things with a couple as broadminded as Darren and Marcia was beyond tempting.

Charlotte climbed into the car.

Tom and Judy
David Hawthorne

I have fucked my share of married women; some of them I met at the same bar where my friend Tom asked me to meet him. A lot of women came here after work and it's pretty easy to strike up a conversation while they sip their wine and enjoy my attention. Over the years, I have developed a sixth sense and can tell when these lonely ladies want something other than just a drink.

Until now all of my encounters with married women had been on the sly without hubby knowing that his sweet little lady just put out for another cock. Most of the time, the women I hook up with are simply looking for something they are not getting at home. Either hubby is working too hard or is too busy playing golf to pay them much attention. I've even had a few tell me they are just getting even with their husbands who they found out were screwing around with their secretaries.

This situation was different. Tom and I have known each other for a long time and see each other almost every day. We work at different companies but have lunch together on occasion and share a mutual interest in sports. I have even been invited to his home many times. His wife, Judy, is a knockout, in my humble and correct opinion. I have to admit that I have had my share of lustful thoughts about her but had never given a thought to trying anything.

Tom fished out a packet of photos from his jacket pocket and showed them to me. In every photo, his lovely wife Judy was wearing some very sheer lingerie or was completely nude. He exuded a great deal of pride as he shared the photos with me. Some of the photos clearly showed Judy's beautiful breasts with large pink nipples and some displayed her trimmed pussy and swollen pussy lips. There is not a man in this world that would not jump at the chance to fuck this beautiful woman.

'A few years ago, I began to read and hear about couples that brought a male partner into their relationship,' Tom said. 'When I first suggested having another man join us in our bedroom, Judy seemed shocked but it was obvious to me that she was open to the idea. During the past month or so, I have brought the subject up a few more times during our lovemaking. A couple of nights ago, I talked about it again, and this time she just looked me right in the eye and asked when I was going to do something about it.'

'There must be a lot of men that you know who could be a candidate *and* who would love to make your fantasy a reality. She's a very attractive woman. How did I get so lucky?'

'I have thought about asking some of our friends but Judy wasn't interested in any of them. I know she likes you and has even mentioned your name during some of our lovemaking sessions. There is also one very distinctive difference in you!'

'Oh yeah, what's that?' I said, suddenly curious.

'During all of our fantasies, Judy has consistently fantasised about fucking a man with a really big cock.'

I recalled an incident or two in the restroom when I was taking a leak. Tom was in the next stall and I had caught him looking rather carefully at my cock. I had some uncomfortable feelings but now I understood why he had done it.

'I guess I should be flattered,' I said. 'Thanks, old sport.'

The conversation and the photos were getting me excited and I felt my cock growing harder as Tom told me about Judy's fantasy of being fucked by another guy with a big dick. Mine certainly is in the 'larger-than-average' category at eight thick inches. Soft it's nearly six inches and hard there have been times I thought it reached nine. Sometimes it's the girth more than the length; a few of the women I've known have found it impossible to take it all comfortably. None has ever complained that it wasn't enough.

'Next week is our tenth anniversary,' Tom said. 'We always get a hotel room downtown and go out for a nice dinner and dancing. This year, I thought that you might be a great anniversary present for her. What I really want, buddy, is to watch – watch her get fucked by another guy, watch her take a dick bigger than mine, watch as another man stuffs his sperm in her cunt and mouth ...'

Tom and I agreed how I would 'accidentally' meet them in the dance club that they would go to after dinner. We carefully worked out how we would get things going and how Tom expected Judy to react.

We parted, both of us feeling extremely excited about the game of kink we had hatched.

The plan was for me to be at the club by nine and sit at the bar. Tom and Judy were supposed to arrive a few minutes later. At exactly nine, I walked into the bar and located a spot that gave me a good view of the entire room, ordered a drink and eagerly awaited their arrival.

I spotted Tom coming through the door. It took me a few seconds to recognise his wife. Judy had her hair done differently than I recalled from the photos or the few times I'd seen her at their home. Instead of it hanging down so that it framed her face, she had it swept up and swirled on top of her head. She was wearing a long black dress that fit like a glove, and had a tantalising slit up one side that nearly reached the top of her thigh. The effect was stunning and the anticipation of fucking her left me momentarily breathless.

I watched her ass as they made their way across the room to a table. She was truly one incredible sexy female. As I watched them, I rehearsed the plan in my mind. I was to wait fifteen minutes or so, then walk over and say hello. Tom would act surprised to see me but would invite me to join them.

As I excitedly waited the appropriate amount of time, they ordered their drinks. Martini for Judy and Scotch on the rocks for Tom. After the waitress delivered the drinks, I walked across the room to their table.

'Hey, look who's here,' I said to Tom. 'I didn't know you came here. It's a great club, isn't it?'

Tom acted surprised to see me. 'Hey! What the hell are you doing here?' he said, shaking my hand. 'You remember my wife, Judy?'

'I must admit you look even lovelier than I remembered,' I said, taking her hand and kissing it.

'Why, thank you, Steve,' she replied with a warm smile.

'Are you here alone?' Tom asked, pretending to look around the room.

'Sure am,' I replied. 'Just stopped by to have a quick drink before heading to my dull apartment.'

'Would you like to join us for a drink?' he asked, glancing at Judy for approval.

I accepted the invitation and sat down next to Judy. We made small talk for a few minutes before Tom took Judy to the dance floor. Everything was going exactly as planned. Tom was going to bring her back to the table as soon as the DJ played a slow song. That would be my cue to invite her to dance. I had worn jockey shorts that held my cock up even when it was soft. I also wore rather tight-fitting slacks that would make my package quite noticeable when I pressed against her body.

Tom and Judy returned to the table as planned. I waited an appropriate minute or two before making my move. I turned to Tom and said, 'Say, old sport, if you're not going to dance with this beautiful lady, would you mind if I do?'

'Be my guest,' he replied.

I didn't want to scare her off right away so I made a point of dancing with some space between us. Despite the minimal distance, I could feel her body gently brushing against my cock, which was starting to enlarge, but she showed no reaction. I figured everything was all right; she was comfortable with it.

'Thank you, Judy,' I said, as we returned to the table when the tempo picked up again.

'You're an excellent dancer,' she replied sweetly.

I went to the bar and ordered another round of drinks for us all. We sat and chatted for a while. Judy sipped her drink and acted coy, like she knew what we had in mind and she was simply waiting for the game to begin. Tom and I discussed the stock market ups and downs and the current scores of our favourite football teams, then Tom and Judy went back to the dance floor and remained there for two rather fast rockabilly songs. When another slow song came on, they returned and it was time to put the next part of the plan into action.

'Judy, may I have the pleasure again?' I said.

Without answering, she held out her hand and I led her back to the dance floor. This time, I held her a little closer but still not too conspicuously tight. I knew that she could feel the lump of my cock as it happily rubbed against her. I pulled her closer and she didn't resist or push me away. Her body pressed against mine and I could feel my cock start to expand. Unfortunately, the song tempo changed again before things got very far and we returned to the table. Tom and Judy took to the floor again and I could see Judy whispering in Tom's ear as they danced. They returned after just one dance and Judy excused herself to go to the powder room.

Tom slammed his hand on the table excitedly and told me that Judy had noticed my cock while we were dancing. 'I didn't know you had a porn-star cock.'

'She wasn't upset, was she?' I asked. 'I tried not to be too obvious.'

'Oh no, in fact, she's rather intrigued by it. I think it won't be long before she will be begging to try it out.'

'I'm ready any time she is.'

'So am I,' Tom said.

As Judy returned to the table, the music switched to another slow number. This time, I simply reached for her hand before she sat down. We moved to the music and I pulled her close. I dropped my hand to her ass and pressed my cock deliberately against her. She responded by pushing firmly against me, allowing her body to massage my cock until it grew about as big as it would ever get. Putting her head on my shoulder, she snuggled against me. Her breath came in rapid gasps. 'Am *I* causing that?' she whispered in my ear. 'I've never felt anyone quite so *big*.'

'I think he likes you,' I whispered back. 'He only gets this way when I am with an exceptionally sexy woman. I hope you don't mind because I can't do very much about it when I'm holding you this close.'

'I don't mind,' she said. 'I'm flattered. I mean it feels so *nice*. I've never had the chance to enjoy anyone this hung. I know I shouldn't say this, especially on our anniversary, but if Tom weren't here I would take you up to our room and fuck you so hard your dick would have to take a week off.'

It was clear Judy was ready. I led her back to the table, and, as we sat down, she moved her chair a little closer to mine and I felt her hand slyly massage my erection. She tried to look as if nothing was happening but when Tom spoke to her she didn't seem to hear him. I reached over and slipped my hand through the slit of her skirt and began to work my way up to her pussy. I could feel her warmth when I was inches away, even before I got to her panty-covered cunt. She squirmed when I touched her there. Her panties were soaking wet.

She definitely was ready and I said, 'Tom, I think your wife is prepared to receive her special present.'

Tom, who had been observing everything we were doing, simply nodded.

'What are you two talking about?' Judy said.

Tom leaned over the table. 'Sweetheart, I have arranged a *very special* present for you, on our anniversary.'

She wasn't sure what to say or how to react. 'How sweet.'

'*Steve* is your anniversary present. He is going to come with us to our room and give you the opportunity to enjoy a great present: that monster between his legs.'

She blushed.

'Do you like my present?' her husband asked.

She nodded, squeezing my cock.

Their hotel was a short walk away and Tom and I both had our arms around her as we walked. Every other step she would let her hand rub across the bulge in my pants. By the time we reached the hotel, I was so turned on and ready that the minute we were in the elevator I pulled her to me and kissed her passionately. She dropped her hand to my crotch and tried to pull my zipper down. Once she had it down as far as it would go, she pushed her hand inside and tried unsuccessfully to pull my cock out. But I was so hard and she was unable to free it. Tom watched us with a 'my-wife's-about-to-get-fucked-by-another-man' grin on his mug; it was an attitude that I was quickly beginning to like and comprehend.

We walked down the corridor to their room and she was still trying to extract my cock. I glanced over at Tom who was watching her every move. As soon as we entered their room, she dropped to her knees and quickly unfastened my belt and pulled my slacks down.

'It's gorgeous, absolutely *gorgeous*!' she blurted.

She took the head in her mouth and swirled her tongue around it. Tom was sitting on the edge of the bed, having found the best vantage point to observe the action, an expression of delight on his face as his wife lovingly sucked his friend's cock. I knew she wouldn't be able to take it all in but she was a trooper and tried.

Tom removed his clothes and I took off my shirt, leaving Judy the only one still fully dressed. Tom unzipped the back of her dress, and, as she continued to lap and lick and kiss and spit on my cock, he slid the dress over her arms and down her body, leaving her in black bra, panties, garter belt and hose.

'You are an incredibly beautiful and sexy woman,' I said.

She liked those words, all women do. I unsnapped her bra. She held her arms to her sides and let it fall away. Her tits were even better than the photos and I caressed them as Tom slid her panties down and let them fall to the floor. She took my hand and led the way to the bed where she fell backwards and spread her legs apart revealing her neatly shaved pussy. She held her arms outstretched, inviting me to her body. I was treated to a great view of her pink glistening slit.

She was ready all right.

I had to taste her exquisitely sexy cunt first, and fell to the floor and buried my head between her legs. The warmth and smell of her pussy made my cock throb in anticipation. Bending closer, I slid my tongue over her wet sex, causing her to jump and press her pelvis to me. Her body quivered and shook as her first climax of the evening surged like a tsunami.

She said, 'I want you to fucking fuck me now. Please put that fucking cock in me and fuck me hard, please.'

I wanted to make sure that Tom got the full visual effect of my cock entering his wife's cunt so I raised her leg and moved it out of the way. I rubbed the head up and down her slit to get it well lubricated. Tom stopped stroking himself and leaned forward to watch as my dick penetrated his loving wife.

Both Judy and Tom gasped as I pressed forward and went inside. I was about halfway in when I heard Tom groan. I looked over to witness a blast of come shooting from his cock, a long white stream that went up and arched, before hitting the edge of the bed. Judy seemed oblivious to her husband's ejaculation. I slowly pushed forward and buried all eight inches into her. I held it there to allow her body to adjust, then slowly withdrew until just the tip was embedded.

'Please don't fucking tease me, please,' she cried, begging. 'I want you to fucking fuck me. Fuck me fucking hard. I want that big fucking cock fucking deep inside my fucking cunt.'

Many of the women I had bedded in the past were vocal but not like this. Her words turned me on all the more.

My balls slapped her ass as our tempo increased. I felt Tom's movement behind me and looked to see that he was now standing right next to me, watching wide-eyed at the vision of his spouse getting a royal fucking. He stood there mesmerised for several minutes and moved towards the other side of the bed. He guided his cock to her mouth.

'Do me doggie!' she gasped and she turned over and supported herself on her knees and hands. I guided my cock back to her gaping pussy and she took Tom's cock back into her mouth.

She seemed to freeze in mid-stroke and her body shook violently. She screamed as her climax shattered her reality like a plate dropped and broken.

'I fucking love your fucking cock, I love fucking it,' she chanted.

It was my turn. I thought of pulling out and having her suck me, swallow my load, but it was too late, I shot deep in her cunt.

Looking at the juncture where our loins joined, I spied a river of come running around my cock and flowing down her legs. We remained coupled for several moments as my cock slowly returned to its normal size. I gently pulled out. Tom let out a loud gasp as he watched a river of come quickly, thickly run down his wife's leg and on to the bed sheets.

Needless to say, for the next few hours Tom and I happily did everything we could do to satisfy his sex-crazed wife. We made love in every imaginable position. I was able to get off twice more and then I had to surrender to emptiness and fatigue.

Spending the entire night with them was not part of the plan. I woke up in the middle of the night and decided it was time for me to depart, the 'walk of shame' as the booty-callers call it.

I got up quietly and went to the bathroom to wash

off the dried juices of debauchery. I returned to retrieve my clothes and found Judy awake and waiting for me.

She quickly pulled me to the bed where I easily slipped into her wet and willing cunt for yet another round. This time, it was slow and lasted for several minutes before we both reached the peak and experienced another mind-blowing orgasm. Tom had watched us the whole time, lying still and quiet next to us. He did not fuck his wife when I was done; he fell asleep, and so did Judy and I.

That morning, my visit with them was capped off by fucking Judy one last time in the shower while Tom sat on the toilet and watched and jerked himself off.

'You can go now,' Tom said. 'Old sport.'

I looked at Judy and I could see in her eyes that she didn't want me to depart but she nodded her head and said, 'Thank you for a wonderful birthday present.' She looked over at Tom. 'Thank you both.'

Now it did seem like a walk of shame. I got dressed and left them alone.

I never heard from either of them – not a call, an email, a text or a tweet. Our paths crossed briefly at a big Christmas party and they both acted like I didn't exist, but, when Tom wasn't looking, Judy turned and gave me a quick glance like she wanted to get me under the mistletoe or run off with me to never-never land.

I just looked away.

I'll Have What She's Having
Rachel Kramer Bussel

Some restaurants hire professional greeters, buy advertising, offer two-for-one deals or make outrageous dishes designed to lure in tourists and those craving the latest culinary concoctions. I didn't do any of those things when I opened Sizzle, but I did hire Pam after watching from two tables over as she dined with her boy toy, Brad, one afternoon over a particularly languorous brunch at a low-key bistro I frequent. It was a holiday weekend and most New Yorkers were away so I got to stare at her as she consumed a meal fit for a king – or a person twice her size. A fluffy omelette was brought out, along with a side of bacon, followed by a fruit and cheese plate and waffles. Brad was sipping a cup of coffee and nibbling on a Danish, but, like me, mostly he was watching Pam.

92

And no, she didn't go in the bathroom and puke any of it up.

What Pam did was eat her meal with more gusto and sex appeal than I'd ever witnessed anyone consume anything. She had a serene glamour to her, and each bite of every single dish was savoured obsessively, in the manner of a true foodie, with her eyes closed, her head tilted slightly, like the food was taking her to another planet, or maybe another dimension. She wasn't so much ignoring Brad as giving every ounce of her attention over to the meal. The chef in me was riveted, and the man in me was very, very aroused.

I wasn't the only one staring. Brad, who I'd later meet, eventually gave up on his Danish, as Pam gave a performance that would've gotten Meg Ryan replaced on the set of *When Harry Met Sally*. Her sleek black bob shimmered in the light playing off her pale skin, her eyes were closed and her head tilted back so we could practically see the food being swallowed. A quick survey of the room proved that many other diners had found their afternoon's entertainment, right in front of them, at no extra cost.

When Pam paused to take a sip from her lemonade, she used a straw, sucking from it in a way that made her cheeks pull in and intimated what she'd look like with her mouth stuffed full of cock. Whether she was trying to attract attention or not, Pam had almost all the eyes in the restaurant on her – I saw a waiter drop a whole tray of empties as he turned back for just one more peek at her.

Sizzle was all about the hot, the new, the now. I not only wanted the food to be spicy, bold and edgy, but also to have the restaurant itself stand out in any way it could, from the flashing neon pink sign outside to the black-and-white decor inside. I wanted it to be a place where one could see and be seen, where the surroundings were as noteworthy as the food.

I approached Pam when Brad went to the restroom. 'Hi,' I said, slipping her a card. 'I'd like to hire you to work at my new restaurant.' I put my hand up and cleared my throat. 'Before you object, let me assure you I don't mean as a server or hostess. Those jobs would not come anywhere close to maximising your talents. I want you to be the centrepiece of the restaurant, a bit of advertising genius. Your job will be to eat, just like you did today. If you didn't know already, everyone in here was staring at you. They were drawn to you. I want you in my prime window seat, looking sexy and glam and powerful and hungry. All you have to do is eat, slowly and deliberately. Think of it as performance art, if you'd like, and feel free to dine with whomever you like as long as you are constantly putting something in that beautiful mouth of yours. Your boyfriend is more than welcome,' I concluded, even though, if I were to be honest, I already wanted her mouth for myself.

I finished my pitch in a rush of words and then realised I hadn't even told her my name. 'I'm Alan Oliver, by the way.'

'He's not my boyfriend, just a man with a very beautiful cock I like to play with. And yes, I recognise you,' she said, and didn't need to elaborate; I'd done a few stints on *Top Chef* and was hoping to ride that buzz for my latest endeavour. 'Well, apparently this is my lucky day. I just got fired from my design job and have been trying to figure out where to go next, not to mention stocking up on pasta and peanut butter. This was a little escape. I'm familiar with your work. I'm into the idea … but this sounds a little outrageous. How much would I have to eat? I don't want to get fat.' She managed to say all of that, from 'cock' to 'fat', without losing an ounce of her calm assurance.

'I'll buy you a gym membership, and we'll do small plates, whatever you'd like, on the menu or off.'

After just a little negotiating, I hired Pam for a regular forty-hour workweek, telling her she should bring a guest, unless I'd lined someone up, so it wouldn't look odd to see such a gorgeous woman dining alone repeatedly. I placed her in the prime seat from day one; she was our first customer, much to the chagrin of an eager-beaver middle-aged balding foodie who showed up right on the dot of eleven on opening day, tossing a look Pam's way as if to say, 'Who'd she blow to get that table?' The truth was, all she'd blown on was the steaming bowl of cauliflower soup I'd just served her along with a salmon tartar salad and glass of jalapeño lemonade. Her friend Andrea joined her soon thereafter, dressed in an orange pantsuit that billowed, drawing even more attention.

I didn't have time to stare at Pam every minute, but I could tell that just having her in place was enough to draw curious passers-by from the street, and to keep their attention once they entered. If a woman as beautiful and glamorous as Pam was glued to her seat, with waiters serving up seemingly non-stop delights to her table, they might just have to check out the hot new restaurant for themselves. Brad joined her for dinner and I watched her lean back while he cut her steak, a move of either gentlemanly deference or submissive training. Either way, it made her power over me complete.

The place filled up quickly that first day and soon we were booked a week in advance. As we got into the swing of things, I let Pam rotate her position, trying out the bar and other seats, but wherever she was, she failed to blend. She stood out even when she switched her normally bright red lipstick for a pale pink or retro white. She had the magic touch, and the gossip columns were even starting to wonder who exactly this elegantly appointed, sexy middle-aged woman with the black bob, designer outfits and non-stop appetite was. She made it into Page Six with a cup of Starbucks coffee and doughnut in her hand: SIZZLE STYLE MAVEN SLUMS IT read the headline. My plan had worked! Of course, maybe Sizzle would've been a stunning success without Pam – I'll never know – but with her there, I not only had an on-demand food tester but the most gorgeous eye candy I could imagine, something that came in handy after a long day putting out fires, literal and otherwise.

One day I got an unexpected request. An older businessman, his salt-and-pepper hair and deeply tanned skin probably putting him at sixty, asked if Pam was available as a dining companion. 'What do you mean?' I replied, trying to play it cool. Was it that obvious that she was an employee rather than simply a very enthusiastic customer? And exactly what kind of companion did he have in mind?

'Well, I've seen her here every time I've walked in and she looks like she'd be a delight to dine with. I'd pay for the meal, and for her time. That's all I want, truly. I'm divorced and don't tend to meet women so easily these days.' His look turned urgent. 'I've never done anything like this before, but I'm drawn to her. I watch her every time I eat here and, well, let's just say it's enhanced my dining experience.' I let my eyes roam out the doorway to survey the room and indeed, most of the men and many of the women were watching Pam, their gazes flickering towards her as she consumed each bite as if it were her last, her only. She ate everything from her spicy shrimp gazpacho to her poached halibut to her lemon meringue tart and fruit and cheese plate with a theatrical flourish. My own cock twitched as she speared a raspberry with a fork and popped it between her lips. She smiled at me as if we shared a secret as she sprinkled some sugar on her strawberries.

'Excuse me for a moment.' Her friend had left before dessert, so I was able to catch Pam alone.

'You're a very popular girl tonight. That man in my office wants to have dinner with you. Right here, right now. Well, I'm pretty sure he wants to do more than have dinner with you, but that's what he's asking.'

'So I'm good at oral, is that what you're saying?' She laughed loudly enough to fill the space around her, and let me see her tongue stained slightly red. 'Don't worry, I'm not going to say no. I'm happy to have some company. Brad found someone a little more available. But I think this calls for a special request from the kitchen.'

'Anything you like, my dear.' Her brown eyes twinkled at me, flirting. I knew she knew I was hard; the truth was I hadn't fucked anyone since I'd hired her. While in the kitchen dreaming up new recipes, I'd picture her eating them, or rather, picture me feeding them to her, picture that orgasmic look on her face when she tasted something truly divine.

'I'm pretty easy, actually,' she said. 'I'd like some turkey meatballs in spicy tomato sauce, a side of your wonderful sautéed spinach, wasabi mashed potatoes and then a rich dark chocolate mousse for dessert.'

'I don't know if I'd ever call you easy, Pam, but that is certainly something I can whip up.' One thing I'd come to appreciate about Pam's palate was that she was game for trying my most ambitious concoctions, and would give me her honest opinion, while maintaining a poker face as she sat in public, but could appreciate hearty, homespun meals as well.

'What's the man's name?'

'Peter,' I said, then paused. 'You don't have to do this, Pam. It's not in your job description.'

She took out a compact and sheer lip gloss, which I'd seen her apply repeatedly over the course of the last month; she'd told me she used a long-lasting lipstick to keep her lips red throughout her meals. 'I know I don't have to. I want to. I like eating the food you make. Even when you just tell someone else to make it.' The look she gave me pierced me; she was clearly saying so much more. 'Maybe we could eat together sometime. Not here, not a work thing,' she said. 'I could even cook.'

I walked closer, the hum of the restaurant fading in the background. 'I'd like that very much,' I said, longing to touch her shiny hair for myself, finally, to get lost in those glorious lips. At first, yes, I'd pictured her on her knees, using those lips to take my cock between them, but after watching how she held herself, my thoughts had drifted. Now I wanted to taste her, kiss her, devour her all over.

First, though, I had to take care of my customer. I returned and told Peter that Pam would be happy to dine with him, then relayed her requested menu. 'That sounds wonderful,' he said, his eyes taking on a far-off look.

'No funny business,' I warned, even though it wasn't my place to dictate that, especially if they left together. I hoped it would come across sounding protective, paternalistic even, rather than perverse. I was her boss, nothing else, yet it felt like a more intimate relationship. I'd spent so many stolen moments staring at her as I surveyed Sizzle or sat taking a meeting, my gaze drifting towards her. She was never overly loud, and even those times when she should've blended with the rest of the crowd, she never did, not for me. Without being overly dramatic, she still managed to command attention, as if she were sending out signals to other diners to indicate that they may be sharing the same food, but she was enjoying it infinitely more than they were.

'I wouldn't dream of it. I'll leave her to you,' Peter said with a knowing look. OK, my jig was up, but I would still get the pleasure of watching the two of them together. Never had my voyeuristic side been quite so engaged as it was when I watched Pam – and watched others watching her. It was a ripple effect, and seeing the joy she brought others not only enhanced our collective dining experiences, but made her seem like a special prize, a woman whose lips were in much demand.

I oversaw the preparation of the meal, whipping up the special sauce myself, adding some rare spices for a kick I knew Pam would appreciate. As I tasted my red bubbling concoction, I wished it were me sitting across from her, feeding her, watching so many emotions play across her face as she dined. I set the dish of meatballs, the sides, along with the mashed potatoes, on a tray and brought it over myself. There was a smile on Pam's face already that caused me to look below the table; they were playing footsie!

Rather than be jealous, though – after all, I was twenty years younger than Peter and ran my own set of successful restaurants – I was again aroused by proxy. 'Thank you,' they both said at the same time, and I was forced to retreat. I went into my office and watched on the hidden camera I'd installed; I wouldn't go so far as to record conversations, but I had the pleasure of seeing Pam's face in black and white as she dished out meatballs, mashed potatoes, and spinach evenly among the two plates. She nodded her head to indicate he should eat first.

Then Pam cocked her head slightly, awaiting her companion's impression. Only after he smiled did Pam set about starting her meal, while I again marvelled at her stomach's ability to put away enough food for three women and still remain trim. As she ate, I watched closely.

She lacked a poker face, so each mouthful made a signifi-cant impression on her face and, when she closed her eyes, it was clear she was trying to deconstruct the meal in her mouth, to break it down to its component parts, solve the culinary mystery even as she savoured the mix of textures and flavours. I wondered what she would taste like; I'd been close enough to smell her coconut-scented skin a few times, but what about her lips, her tongue, her mouth, her sex? Were they warm and spicy and delicate like flowers? Was she reminiscent of our chilled cucumber soup or more like our mole sauce?

I found my hand going to my cock, grateful for the privacy of the small room, as I watched her taste each and every part of the meal. When she held a forkful of spinach up to her nose and simply sniffed, I was a goner. I came in my hand, then looked around for a way to clean up.

I wiped my hand on a towel and pressed the intercom to tell Greg, my most handsome waiter, to serve the dessert. I'd made extra chocolate mousse, not because I had anything close to an appetite, but because I hoped she'd like it and would want more.

Finally, their meal was over, which was my cue. I went to shake Peter's hand, telling him the meal was on the house. He looked like he was in a food coma, his eyes slightly glazed over, as he thanked me profusely and promised to return very soon.

Dinner hour was winding down and Pam's official duties were over. I hoped she would still want to share herself with me. 'Well, you sure do know how to follow orders, Alan,' she said.

'I do?'

'Yes. Maybe you're so used to giving them that you know what it's like. What I'm trying to say is the food was delicious.' She just sat there, smiling at me. 'But I think you're going to have to fire me. Because otherwise we might wind up engaging in some improper workplace behaviour.'

'Like what?' I asked like an idiot. I thought she wanted to cook for me at her place.

'I can't wait,' she said, as if reading my mind. 'I want you now. Sit down.' Even though we were still open, I followed her command. 'I'll have to cook for you another time. Right now, I want to watch you, since you've been so studiously watching me. Yes, I've noticed.' She laughed, a sound that immediately cut me down to size – but didn't cut down on my erection in any way.

She then signalled a waiter and reeled off the priciest dishes on my menu, including the $50 hamburger – not that I cared. I'd happily pay just to be in her company. I could feel the stares of everyone around us. Then I felt her foot in my lap. 'Rub my feet while we wait. I want you to be on display for a change. I've been thinking about what you look like naked ... maybe coated in chocolate mousse. What a pretty picture that makes,' Pam said, her voice dreamy with desire. 'And by the way, I want a raise. I know exactly what's going on here, and I think your business would go way down if I wasn't sitting here doing my best to eat as slowly as humanly possible. Don't get me wrong, your food is divine, but still, a girl wants something else in her mouth once in a while.'

I tried to focus on her feet, on digging my knuckles into her skin, wanting to see if I could make her lose her cool, even just for a minute. I knew that even though we were mostly hidden, there was still an air of danger in what I was doing; should someone notice my hands moving, or pick up on the sexual tension between us, I could be in trouble – but Pam was worth it. Instead of breaking her calm, though, she just stared at me. The burger arrived but I had no appetite, not for food, but I couldn't refuse it without losing her and looking like I was the type of chef who preferred McDonald's. Under her gaze, I lifted the burger, realising this was the first time I'd truly gotten to sit in my own restaurant and relax. Well, relax may be overstating it, because my senses were on high alert, but I wasn't thinking business, just pleasure.

I had to shut my eyes eventually as her stare became too intense – and because her foot was pressing against my cock. I took several slow bites of the burger, relishing the mix of tastes on my tongue. When I opened my eyes, she was offering me a fry and licking her lips. This was food as foreplay, no doubt about it. Disregarding everything around me, I let her feed me, her fingers brushing my lips and tongue.

I was sure everyone had to be watching us when that happened, because even that simple act Pam managed to imbue with so much eroticism I felt like I was eating something much more sensual than a fried potato. She savoured the act as much as she savoured each bite of food, making each second count. I was suddenly sure that even if someone were watching us, like Peter my customers would fall under Pam's spell just as surely as I had.

'How do you like it, Alan? How do you like having everyone watch every bite you eat, thinking about your mouth, what it takes like, how warm and wet it is? I know that's what you think about. I see you watching me.'

'I like it,' I said. 'I mean, I like you. I've wanted you since that first day I talked to you. I'll fire you if I have to. I just want to taste you, to smell you, to savour you.' I couldn't hold the burger in my shaking hands so I sliced off a piece to stuff in my mouth before I embarrassed myself further.

Pam signalled over her head and soon my plates were being whisked away and Greg was saying, 'I'll take care of things, sir.' How she had signalled all of this to him with a wave of her fingers, I didn't know, but I followed her out.

She didn't speak to me as we walked two blocks to a high-end hotel, where, after requesting a room with a window facing the busiest street, she stepped aside and I whipped out my credit card. She handed me her purse to carry, even though it was a light one; I'd have crawled on my hands and knees to follow her into the room. Turns out, Pam's an attention-magnet even when she's not eating. She slipped the key card in the door and the minute it was closed she had me on my knees right in front of the giant glass window. We were on the sixth floor, high enough that probably no one could see us very closely, but low enough that they could guess what was going on. 'Put your hands behind your head. I just want your mouth, the way you just wanted mine,' she said.

Then she hiked up her skirt and pushed down her black mesh lace panties. I barely had a minute to glimpse the strip of dark pubic hair against her pale skin before she was straddling my face and giving me the meal that had inspired my cooking ever since we'd met. No, none of my dishes were exactly reminiscent of the slippery wetness of her pussy, of the salty tang of her sex, but the tingling I felt on my tongue and throughout my body was exactly what I'd been looking to evoke with my menu. Pam grabbed my short hair and rammed my tongue deeper into her. 'Harder,' she commanded.

That made sense; a woman like Pam wouldn't want a slow, sensual licking, the way she took her time eating the food I prepared for her. She was done being slow, and so was I. I grabbed her hips and sucked her clit between my lips, then my teeth, loving the way she trembled above me. Now she was holding on to me so she wouldn't fall, and I dared add a finger to my oral explorations, followed by two. Soon my tongue was slithering into her cunt along with my fingers, when I wasn't feasting on her clit. Her hand moved to my cheek, slapping me and making me almost come in my pants.

When she realised how much I liked it, she kept slapping me, even going so far as to ease my face out from between her legs so she could look at my glossy lips and give my cheek the full force of hand. The thought of a stranger seeing that through the window made my whole body buzz with excitement. It's one thing to be owned by a woman, to be fully at her mercy, but it's another thing to have the whole world, or even a slice of it, know that. I'm not sure how many times I made her come, only that each climax worked its way through my body too, from my nose to my lips on down. I shuddered right alongside her, my mouth glued to her until she finally pushed me away.

'Now for dessert,' she said, and proceeded to drag me

by my cock over to the full-length closet mirror. She took it out and we both watched in the mirror as she wrapped her hand around my shaft and jerked it with firm, even strokes. She put my hand where hers had been and then took off her blouse and bra, leaving her natural breasts hanging there, the nipples hard and firm. She wrapped her breasts around my hardness and I was soon enveloped in the softness of her beautiful flesh. When she told me to come, I had no choice, even though I could've stayed in that glorious position for hours, it seemed. I watched as my cock let out streams of white cream all over her breasts, painting them. And then she stood and once again brought my head down, this time to lick up my own come. I'd fed it to girls, the horny kind who got off on it, before, and had taken a stray taste or two, but had never been with a woman like Pam, one who was adamant about me being an equal opportunity come drinker. I licked off every drop until her breasts were again bare, with only traces of my saliva to show what we'd just done.

She hummed to herself as she got dressed. 'I'm going to keep the job. But I want my own menu item. I want to share myself with your customers. I want you to call it, "I'll Have What She's Having". I want it to be something so rich, so amazing, so much of an aphrodisiac that it'll make them have a mouth orgasm and be so turned on they'll have to leave as soon as they finish it.'

'It's a deal,' I said, before rushing back to the restaurant, which my staff had locked up for me, in order to concoct my most perfect recipe yet.

Remote Access
Elizabeth Coldwell

What do I do for a living? I sit on things. Usually in a bikini. Oh, my official job title is promotions girl, but that's really just a fancy name for sitting on top of a car and smiling.

I know what you're thinking. I'm some kind of silicone-enhanced bimbo who's setting back the sisterhood by using my body rather than my brains to make money. Not only that, I haven't got the wits to see I'm being exploited every time I shimmy into a swimsuit no larger than a couple of handkerchiefs tied together and sprawl across the bonnet of the latest top-of-the-range SUV. But, while it's true my breasts are round and very full, they're entirely natural, as are my big curvy bottom and wasp waist. The kind of body that rules me out of fashion modelling but has men falling over themselves to pay it compliments. I've always had more attention lavished on my tits than my face, so I decided I might as well get paid for it – and paid handsomely at that. Which begs the question, who's exploiting who?

That's not to say it doesn't get tedious when some middle-aged middle manager's eyes are practically burning holes in my knickers, or a sweaty sales rep 'accidentally' grabs a handful of my breast while he's reaching for a promotional leaflet. It's not in the rules to rake your stilettos down their shins, otherwise more than a few of the punters I meet in my average working day would be going home with heel marks gouged in their flesh.

And some assignments are better than others. Sometimes I'm asked to distribute flyers at exhibitions. The outfits I wear on those occasions are slightly less revealing – usually a T-shirt advertising the company I'm working for, knotted under my breasts to reveal my smooth honey-tanned midriff, and a pair of skimpy buttock-skimming shorts – and the perks are better. I've had several hot dates as a result of scribbling my mobile number on the flyer before handing it to the cutest man in the crowd. That, incidentally, is also against the rules, but I haven't been caught yet.

I've even been booked to model at a couple of big fetish events, which proved to be real eye-openers. A few of the girls I know won't touch anything they see as being involved with the sex industry, but the people who attend those events are much more respectful than your average car-show punter, I can tell you. Mind you, when they're being led round on a lead, wearing nothing but a leather jockstrap, by a woman in a black leather catsuit and four-inch heels who will swat their arse with a riding crop if they're disobedient, I don't suppose they can behave any other way.

The first time I worked with a specialist fetishwear designer, I was a little apprehensive, I'll admit. The show was in one of the big exhibition centres in Birmingham, and along with another girl I had the job of wearing three different rubber or PVC outfits during the course of the day. We made a striking couple. Lorelei was a tall slender girl with hair dyed midnight black, dramatically Gothic make-up and rings piercing her eyebrow and lower lip. I was all curves and blonde curls, and the baby-blue rubber dress I was squeezed into strained across my tits. It was Lorelei who taught me the tricks of slipping painlessly in and out of the tight clinging fabric without damaging it. First she dusted the dress with a generous amount of baby powder, and then she dusted my naked body. The first time her hands smoothed over my breasts, her touch was on the professional side of friendly. The second, she spent a little more time than was necessary attending to my nipples, so, by the time I had donned a white dress expressly cut to flatter an hourglass figure like mine, they stood out hard as cherry stones. As for the third time, I'm sure Byron, the designer employing us, must have wondered where we had disappeared to, we were gone for so long. I don't know what he would have said if he'd witnessed Lorelei's hand snaking between my pussy lips to tease my juicy clit while her tongue pressed insistently into my willing mouth, though I'm sure the sight would have had his cock fighting to escape from his PVC trousers.

I'd never kissed anyone with a tongue stud before. Come to that, I'd never let another girl caress my tits and push her fingers up into my cunt before. I leaned back against the wall of the toilet cubicle we were supposed to be changing in, and let Lorelei replace her fingers with that sexy pierced tongue. She went at me with rapid feline licks, lapping at the juices which were seeping down the insides of my thighs. I clutched desperately at the paper dispenser and whimpered as my pleasure built, already too far gone to wonder whether there might be anyone in an adjoining cubicle and what they would think if they could hear us. The feeling when the little chunk of metal embedded in her tongue connected with my clit was so exquisite I couldn't help myself. I threw my head back and squealed as I came. When we returned to the main hall, I made some excuse about having problems with the laces on my corset dress, but I was sure everyone could tell from my

113

pleasure-glazed expression and the unmistakable scent of sex Lorelei and I were giving off what had really happened.

Despite – or maybe because of – my unexpected girl-on-girl interlude, Byron booked me again, for a three-day exhibition in London. His stall was situated on the first-floor gallery of the exhibition hall, not far from where various workshops and performances were scheduled to take place throughout the event. I hadn't realised exactly what some of those performances entailed until three members of an all-male dance troupe walked past on the way to their midday show. They were wearing nothing but black Lycra trunks and heavy boots, and I had never seen so much prime beef in one place: biceps I would have struggled to wrap my fingers around, impossibly ridged stomachs with every single muscle defined and gloriously thick thighs. It was the blond at the head of the party who really captured my attention. His fringe fell into ice-blue eyes, his cheekbones were scalpel sharp – and, as for what he had packed into those tight-fitting trunks, it would have made almost any other man weep with envy. I knew I had to get up close and personal with this slab of masculine perfection, so when he and his friends returned half an hour later, sweat and baby oil glistening on their skin from their exertions, I made sure to wander over and offer him one of Byron's flyers. I knew he wouldn't take it – to be honest, I suspected he would struggle with a word containing as many syllables as 'rubberwear' – but I'd pulled the zip down on my pink-and-black catsuit far enough that my nipples were practically on show. He couldn't resist the bait. Telling Byron I was going to take a short walk to show his stunning creation off to the punters, I gave Blondie a wink and invited him to follow me.

A short walk along the gallery, by a rodeo riding game which had been designed to resemble a giant phallus rather than the usual mechanical bull, was a fire exit leading to a stairwell. We tried the handle and discovered it was open. No one paid us any attention, all far too interested in the antics of the scantily clad brunette who was trying to hang on to the rodeo dildo as it bucked and heaved.

No words were necessary; the second we were through the door, Blondie pressed me up against the wall, scrabbling for the zip on my catsuit. Byron had designed the garment so it unzipped all the way down to the crotch and beyond, otherwise I'd have had one hell of an undignified scramble to get it on and off with the required haste. Blondie spun me round, getting me to hold on to the wooden banister rail. I was leaning forward slightly in my towering platform heels, and I could only imagine the view he was getting of my shaved pussy from behind, its frilly lips protruding lewdly from the rubber, slick with my cream. I looked over my shoulder as Blondie stepped out of his trunks. His cock was every bit the monster his outfit had promised, flopping out as though relieved to be free of its confinement, then swelling to mouth-watering proportions as he tugged at it. He smelled of the strenuous physical workout he'd just gone through, mixed with his own personal musk. While he got himself hard, I fingered my hole, encouraging my juices to flow faster in preparation for taking Blondie's oversized dick.

As wet as I was, I still had a moment as he eased his cockhead into me when I was absolutely certain he wasn't going to fit. I spread my legs wider, pushing back on to the intruder, and felt it nudge its way inside. Though nudge is possibly too subtle a word for Blondie's sexual style. Once he was buried as deep in my cunt as he could go, he gripped my hips and began to thrust into me with the speed and finesse of a pneumatic drill. I clung on to the polished wood for dear life, convinced if he fucked me any harder I would be shunted right out of my heels and over the banister. I couldn't deny Blondie's single-minded intensity wasn't exciting, and, when one of his big manicured fingers slithered down the front of my catsuit and into my pussy, seeking out my clit, I knew he wanted to make sure I got as much pleasure from this as he did.

The squelching noises as his thighs banged against my rubber-clad buttocks and his cock pistoned in and out of my hole were driving us both to distraction. On the other side of the door, I could vaguely hear music coming from the main hall as the hourly fashion show began, coupled with screaming and audience laughter as someone plummeted from the phallic rodeo ride. Those screams were suddenly overlaid with a huge roar from Blondie. He pulled out of me as he came, spattering my catsuit with his thick spunk. My last thought before my own orgasm shot through me was that I would have to buy the outfit now.

By the end of that weekend, I'd not only gained a catsuit – acquired from Byron at a knockdown price, it has to be said – but the man I'm still with now. And no, it wasn't Blondie. Much like the bucking phallus game, one go on that mighty organ was definitely enough. Pretty but stupid isn't a combination that appeals to me long term.

Instead, I found myself swapping phone numbers on the Saturday afternoon with a guy named Richard. With his overlong, mousy hair, silver-framed glasses and lean body in a *Final Fantasy* T-shirt, he was about as far away from Blondie's buff, perma-tanned charms as it was possible to get, but, for some reason, I'm irresistibly attracted to geeks. Show me a man who can work his way round a computer motherboard blindfold and I'm in heaven.

When the show finished on Sunday night and I'd

helped Byron and the other models pack up his few remaining unsold outfits and take down the display items on the stall, I declined the offer to join everyone at the exhibition after-party. I'd made arrangements to see Richard in a pub round the corner, and I had no intention of letting him down.

Soon, I was sitting nursing a very welcome glass of Australian Shiraz and listening enthralled as Richard told me all about his job in tech support for a publishing company, maintaining their networks of PCs. Well, I listened until the moment where I just had to slip off my shoe and tease his crotch with my stockinged toes. I didn't go home with him that night – I was still too sore from my encounter with Blondie the day before to think about fucking anyone else – but within a week we were a couple.

I loved the way Richard had no problems with what I did for a living. Most of the guys I'd started dating after we met in the course of my work claimed they didn't mind me spending all day in my swimwear, but it soon became obvious they hated the thought of other men ogling my body. Never mind the fact they'd ogled it just as hard when they first saw me. Soon they were wishing I'd get some kind of office job or do anything which meant I'd be more covered up. Richard, on the other hand, didn't care who stared at me in the course of my working day because he knew I was coming home to him. Indeed, he kept telling me he wished I could wear something even more revealing – though how it was possible for anything to be more revealing than the teeny-tiny bikini I was expected to wear for the exhibition organised by the team behind *Boy's Toys* magazine I wasn't quite sure.

If you've seen a copy of *Boy's Toys*, you'll know it devotes its pages to gadgets and girls, and every month the staff come up with more inventive ways to combine the two. Richard had long been a regular reader, so when I got the job of modelling on one of their stands he was nearly as excited as I was. I was going to be required to lie on the bonnet of a monster truck wearing a white thong-backed bikini. I knew when I saw it I was going to need the most comprehensive bikini wax of my life, an idea which clearly thrilled Richard. 'Get them to take the whole lot off,' he whispered in my ear as I made the appointment. Happy to tap into what was clearly one of his favourite fantasies, I obliged. Even so, I still thought I looked positively indecent as I tried the bikini on in front of my bedroom mirror, deciding on the accessories which suited it best. The thin white fabric hugged my pussy lips, revealing every contour, and my dark nipples were faintly visible through the top. Richard was hard in his combats just looking at me.

'Are you really sure you're happy with this?' I asked, slipping a heavy silver bangle on to my arm. 'People will be able to see pretty much everything.'

He pulled me against his groin, his rigid erection nestling between my arse cheeks. 'That's the way I like it. You look fantastic, Jay, but it just needs one last accessory.' He held up a smooth egg-shaped piece of plastic.

'And what am I supposed to do with that?' I asked, even though I already knew the answer.

'You wear it for me, all day,' he replied, peeling down the front of my bikini bottoms and slipping the egg up into my pussy.

It wasn't the first time we'd played this kind of game. Richard liked me to go out for an evening with a pair of love balls stuffed in my cunt. They always made me feel more aware than usual of my pussy, as they rolled and clinked together with my movements. This looked much the same, only larger, and I knew how much it would excite Richard to have me on display in that packed exhibition hall with something so rude buried inside me.

As I was running a little late, I didn't bother to change out of the bikini. I just threw my other clothes on over the top and dashed for the tube. Richard had a ticket for the show, and would be coming down for the last couple of hours of the day. There was a strange little smirk on his face as he kissed me and said he would see me later, but I didn't think too much of it at the time.

The *Boy's Toys* show was being held at the big new exhibition centre in the Royal Docks, out beyond the imposing glass and steel towers of Canary Wharf. I was mentally prepared for a long boring day – and that was very much the case until Richard arrived. In the ultra-revealing bikini, it was hard not to be conscious of how I sat down. The back of the thong was like a piece of dental floss disappearing between my cheeks, and I was worried that, if I lay on my front, as I sometimes did when I modelled on a particularly large vehicle, I might inadvertently cause a diplomatic incident.

The love egg in my pussy must have been having some subconscious effect on me, though, because I kept thinking of all the things Richard had said to me about being more daring when I posed. In his ideal world, I'd be topless on the truck, or wearing a sheer fishnet body stocking which made it abundantly clear that my pussy had been shaved clean. He would have me lying with my legs spread widely, or cupping my breasts and offering them to passing punters. The more I weaved these images in my mind, the hornier I became, but unlike the fetish events I'd worked at there were no near-naked hunks wandering around, and, even if there were, I was strictly a one-man woman now I was with Richard.

So when he appeared, round about half past four, and I felt a strange tingling in my sex, I just put it down to all the dirty daydreams I'd been having in his absence. I gave him a little smile, made to sit up from the reclining position I'd been in for the last half an hour or so – and a powerful jolt shot through me, radiating out from my cunt.

The sensation passed, but was followed rapidly by another. It was as though a dial had been turned, bringing my body to buzzing life, and, when I glanced over to Richard, I realised that was exactly what had happened. He flashed me a wicked grin and let me see what he was holding in his palm. I recognised it instantly as some kind of remote-control device, and, as another strong vibration shook me to the core, I knew it had to be coming from the toy he'd inserted there before I left the house.

You dirty, horny bastard, I thought. From the expression on his face, and the way the egg was now vibrating at a constant speed, I knew his exact intentions. To bring me to orgasm in front of everyone crowding round the truck. And the worst part was, I wanted him to do it. Even as I was doing my best to pretend nothing was happening, that my nipples weren't trying to force their way through my bikini top and my pussy juices weren't soaking through the crotch of my bottoms, making them cling even more indecently, I was positively trembling with excitement.

I couldn't stop myself. I went into my best approximation of the splits. It helped the vibrating egg to touch the most sensitive spots on my cunt walls, and it also gave the audience a perfect view of how little the bikini bottoms actually covered. Was it my imagination, or did everyone shuffle a pace closer, fighting to get a better look? When I rolled over so my bare arse was in the air, revealing the way the tiny thong bisected my cheeks and almost, but almost displayed my dimpled arsehole, I could have sworn there was a collective groan of lust.

I didn't want to see their faces as I humped the truck's bonnet, feeling an unstoppable climax building deep inside me. I wanted to imagine them with their zips down and their cocks out, wanking in tribute to my beauty and my wantonness. When they came, their come would rain down on the shiny black paintwork and decorate my voluptuous arse. And my sexy geek of a boyfriend would have made it all happen.

Thinking of Richard, fisting his hard-on along with the rest, I gave up my last shreds of resistance and let my orgasm pound through me, going on and on till I lay sweating and exhausted. If Richard had wanted, he could have cranked up the dial and made me come again, but I suppose he thought I'd put on enough of a performance for one day.

How Richard managed not to get thrown out by security and I kept my job for the rest of the exhibition I'll never quite understand. Presumably everyone who stood round watching enjoyed it far too much to blow the whistle on either of us. Perhaps they were hoping we would come up with another stunt which would top it.

I know Richard is thinking of something even more revealing for my next exhibition. I know his ambition is to find some way of stripping me naked in front of a hall full of salivating punters, all by remote control. And, if he manages to do it, frankly, I'll enjoy every single minute of it. After all, it's all in a day's work.

Revenge
Chrissie Bentley

Oh, we all know guys like Bill. He's God's gift to women, and he doesn't care who knows it. He's got a cock the size of Connecticut, a mouth as wide as the Mississippi, and what he doesn't know about pleasing the babes could be written on the back of a postage stamp. And there's nothing he likes more than sinking a bucket of beer with his buddies, while he regales them with the latest newsflash about his love life.

'Yeah, she was begging for it by the time I was done licking her pussy,' he was saying. 'I had her coming out of her ears, and her ass was bouncing so hard I could have used her as shocks on my Chevy.'

'Did ya fuck her, then?' That was Butch, a rodent-like, pimply little jerk whose parents probably wet themselves laughing when they remember what they named him. Butch? He couldn't fart his way out of a wet paper bag, and you know the only reason Bill kept him around was because an ego can never have too many supporters. Not when it's the size of Bill's, anyway.

He looked up as I walked over. 'Oh, look, it's the Witch Bitch.'

A couple of months back, I'd floated the idea of starting a Wiccan group on campus – and why not? The Catholics had one, the Jews had one, even the Buddhists – all two of them – had one. But the Dean put a stop to that idea, then rewarded me with a lecture on the dangers of Satanism. Which, of course, is precisely the kind of stupidity that I wanted to stomp on by forming the group. But that's just the way of the world. The dumb get dumber and the rest of us better join them, else they'll shoot us while we're sleeping.

It's a small world and a smaller campus. Word got out about my plan, and Bill (of course it was Bill – who else has his erudite way with words?) immediately coined a new name for me. At first it was just 'the Witch'. Then, when I told him where he could stick his wit, his poetic genius added 'Bitch'.

There was more. There was the copy of the 'Witch Bitch Prayer' that was pinned to the noticeboard, a badly typed revision of the Lord's Prayer, spattered with references to Satan and lesbians. Nobody saw who put it there, but how many typewriters were there on campus that didn't have the letter 'e'? Apart from Bill's?

I put my name down for various campus activities. Bill would cross it out. And there was that little incident in my dormitory, where someone jerked off on my pillowcase. Again, nobody actually saw who did it, but why was Bill seen trotting down the back stairs during recess, when nobody else was around?

So, yeah, there was a bit of history here. But it was ending tonight.

I walked over to the pool table, and I was looking fucking hot. Tits tucked high, shorts cut higher. You know what they used to say about English girls' clothing, when the first American servicemen got there during World War Two? 'One Yank and it's off.' My ensemble barely needed a gentle tug, and the best part? I wasn't wearing anything underneath. I was twenty, I was tight in all the right places, and I didn't need the panty lines to add contours to my ass. Yeah, Bill might think he's God's gift to women, but I *know* I was the Goddess' gift to men that night, and I was waving my bounty in his face.

I picked up a cue, stroked my fingers down the shaft. 'So, Billy boy, fancy having your ass whupped tonight?'

'Yeah, right.'

I could feel his little ferrety eyes boring into my cleavage, and I braced my back just a little, to give him a better view.

'Come on. One frame, and, I'll tell you what, winner takes all.' I raised one leg, put my foot on the edge of the table. 'And I mean *all*.' I smiled, and felt all five pairs of eyes staring into my crotch.

'Go on, Bill, you can take her,' said one of his smirking cronies. 'And then you can take her again. Come on, she's offering it to you on a plate.'

Bill was stupid, but he wasn't dumb. 'Yeah, but I don't trust her. She's up to something.'

'You reckon? Or maybe you're just chicken.' I picked up a ball from the table, balanced it on my palm, then traced a fingertip lightly across it.

'Chicken? Around you? Fuck off, Witch Bitch. I just don't trust you, that's all.'

'Yeah, you might turn him into a frog or something,' Butch piped up.

'I might turn you back into a human being if you don't watch yourself,' I snapped back, and there was a laugh from the others, despite themselves. 'So, Bill, are you game? I'll even let you break.'

Bill still looked doubtful, but things had gone too far for him to back out. His pride depended upon it. 'OK. But you heard her, guys. Winner takes all. And I warn you, Witch Bitch, I don't go lightly on anyone.'

'I wouldn't expect you to, champ,' I cooed. 'But I'll warn you, neither do I.'

I'll say one thing for Bill. He's not a bad pool player.

Unfortunately for him, neither am I. Three years hanging with completely the wrong sort of guy (or so my folks used to complain, when I came home with hickeys all over my neck) teaches you a lot of tricks, and playing pool is one of them. So bang-bang-bang and the game was over before Bill was even warmed up.

I stood silently, still stroking my cue; Bill just glowered, while his disciples watched him uncertainly. The guy's an asshole, and he has an asshole's temper. But tonight he simply shrugged. 'Luck. The balls lined up for you. You probably put a hex on them or something.'

It's funny, he ripped seven shades of shit out of me for being a witch, but he certainly didn't have any problem believing it.

'Maybe I did,' I said, smiling. 'But I'll tell you what. We'll play again and, this time, no tricks, no hexes. You up for it?'

Again, he looked uncertain; again, it was the nudging and nods of his crowd that made him back down. 'OK. But someone get me a drink first.'

'Get me one, too,' I snapped. 'Pernod and ice, not too much ice.'

'She even drinks like a fucking witch,' I heard Butch growl. 'What the fuck's Pernod?'

My God, where do these people come from?

This game went much the same as the last, except, this time, Bill barely got started. You know what it's like

129

when every shot you take is the right one, and you've got the ball ricocheting off the cushions, knocking everything down that it's meant to? Even I was surprised how easy it was, and the look on Bill's face was just priceless.

'OK, so winner takes all, right?' I said, as I leaned the cue against the table, then walked around to where Bill was standing.

It was funny, but his crowd all stepped away as I approached, lining up against the wall like they were scared I was going to eat them or something. Which, had they only known, was sort of what I had in mind. But, first, I was going to have my fun.

'OK, all of you, into the Ladies.'

'Fuck you.'

'Not if you don't go into the Ladies, you won't!'

'You're shitting us, right?' Bill had a bit of his old swagger back, although I could see he was still unsure of himself.

I smiled and turned the corner, down the corridor to the bathroom. Behind me, I could hear the others following me.

The ladies' room was immense, twenty stalls, ornate brass fixtures, mirrors that soared to the ceilings. Back in the 1930s, this entire building was a public swimming bath, before a particularly nasty polio outbreak led to it being closed down. It stood derelict for almost forty years, before a guy named Sam bought it and opened a nightclub.

The disco boom died, and the nightclub died with it, so he slowly sold off the rest of the building, and hung on to the foyer and the offices alone. Now it was Sam's, the best bar in town, and the only student hangout where they didn't check ID. Well, Sam's brother was chief of police.

I leaned back against the washbasins, popped a piece of gum in my mouth, and was just about to blow the first bubble when the door swung open and Bill stuck his head round. 'You want to do it in *here*?'

He sounded nervous. 'What's the matter, big boy? Never been in the ladies' room before?'

Behind him, there was a thump and a shuffling as the rest of his pack came to a halt behind him.

'I still want to know what you're up to.'

'Yeah? Well, there's only one way to find out.' I started unbuttoning my blouse, not all the way, but just enough to let my breasts hang free.

There was a sharp intake of breath. 'Christ, look at the tits on that,' came a whisper and I craned my neck to see which of the goblins had said it.

'You wanna piece of them?' I pulled open my blouse. 'They're here. Come and get them.'

Nobody moved. 'Come on, Bill, you're not scared of a pair of old tits, are you? You've sucked on bigger ones than this, I know you have.'

'What if I have?'

'Well, I just want to find out if you're as good at it as you say you are.' I walked over to where he still stood at the door, took his hand and laid it on my left tit. 'See, they don't bite. But do you?'

He gave me a tentative squeeze, and then a slightly firmer one, feeling me up as he sized me up. I looked him in the eye. 'OK, well, you've sampled the goods, now it's my turn.' I reached out and cupped his balls through his jeans. He leaped back as though I'd scalded him; then paused as he caught the eyes behind him. Safety in numbers. 'Come on, you lot, if you're coming in.'

He watched as they pushed in around him … three, four, five of them. Plus Bill, that's six. For the first time, a flicker of doubt ran through my mind. I could take two of them for sure, three if I had to. But half a dozen?

Divide and conquer, and remember who's in charge. I withdrew my hand from Bill's crotch and moved down the line – because that's what they had formed into, a line of nervous raw recruits, with me the sergeant major about to whip them into shape. 'All right, boys, you've seen what I've got. Now let's see yours.'

Hands moved to their collars, unbuttoning shirts.

I shook my head. 'I don't care about that. I want to see downstairs.' And I grabbed the nearest waistline I could, and tugged roughly at the belt. 'Hello, Butch.'

All eyes were on my victim, as I unbuttoned his pants,

unzipped his fly and then, kneeling quickly in front of him, pulled down his trousers and boxers together.

His cock was tiny. Soft and tiny.

I stood. 'Now that's what I want to see. A real man. Come on, fellas, take a look at him. That's a cock and a half if ever I saw one. Or does anyone care to show me a better one?'

I moved to the next boy and repeated the pantomime. 'Oh my, things are really getting steamy now. However can I control my excitement?' And down the line I went, until all five of Bill's friends were standing there sorrowfully, pants around their ankles and their itsy-bitsy inchworms barely popping from their loins.

I stood before Bill. 'But you're going to show us how it's really done, aren't you?' I shrugged off my blouse and laid it on the floor, then knelt down before him, my face at crotch level. 'Come on, Bill, make me beg for it,' I said softly. 'Whip it out and fuck my brains out.'

'Slut,' he muttered under his breath. 'Witchy bitchy slut.'

'That's me. But isn't that how you like your girls? That's how you talk about them, anyway. So, come on, let's see how you treat them. Give us all a show.'

He still wasn't moving, so I did it for him, jerking down his trousers, brushing his bulge with the side of my hand. Well, at least there was something there, this time. I wondered if maybe there was some truth to his tales? But he was clinging on to the waistband of his jockeys, and I knew there was no point playing tug of war with them. So I pointed a finger at his midriff, then traced it down to his cock. Once, twice ... and there was an answering twitch, and the unmistakable quiver of a soft cock unfurling.

'Hey, Bill, where would like to put it? You want it up my ass? My mouth? My pussy? Come on, you're the big man, the hard man, the one who's done it all. Show me what you can do.'

He still wasn't moving, so I raised my voice. 'Show me!'

He raised one leg, and began drawing off his underwear. His cock was half-respectable now, not as big as he'd boasted, but not as small as I'd half-expected. Thick as well, with the kind of fat meaty head that you could use as a war club if it wasn't so soft.

'Now that's better.'

I turned to the others. They were still standing stock still, their eyes firmly fixed on the floor in front of them. 'Take a look, boys. You've heard enough about it, surely you want to see it as well?'

There was an embarrassed shuffling. Somebody coughed.

'Nobody? Never mind, all the more for me, then.'

Back on my knees, I inched closer to Bill, and now I did have their attention. It dawned on me: Bill's stories were probably the closest this crowd had ever come to a real woman before; and now they were about to see for themselves exactly what all the fuss was about.

'Made up your mind yet, Bill? Where you want it?'

'Yeah. I want you to suck on it.' He'd found his voice, and a touch of his old bravado as well.

I leaned forward, holding him firm in my fist, and angled his meat towards my mouth. 'I can do that,' I said sweetly. 'But are you sure you want me to? I have very sharp teeth, you know.'

'Yeah, but you won't use them, will you? Because you want it so much, right? You just want Bill's big old poker down your throat, and you won't stop sucking till you've swallowed all my come.' He turned his head, grinning widely at his mates, as if to say 'I've got her now'. And, when my lips closed over the head of his cock, struggled for a moment to fit it all in, then sucked deep and hard on his hot tangy flesh, I do think he really believed that.

But, hey, he calls me Witch Bitch because he thinks it's clever. I call myself Witch Bitch because it happens to be true. I am a witch, and I am a bitch. And Bill, I'm afraid, is about to find out exactly what that means.

He tasted good. I hate to admit it, because he's such a fucking asshole, but he tasted good, and he felt even better. Fully erect now, his cock had a rare strength; even as I held it down with a fist round the root, I could feel it straining against me, forcing me to adjust my position, straighten my back as I knelt before him, so it could stand at the angle it wanted to. And the helmet! Oh my God, I said it looked meaty, but it felt meaty too, thick and heavy, a bulb of solid manhood that still seemed to be swelling, even now.

For a moment, I thought of abandoning my plan, of just sucking this delicious dick all the way, of taking him to the edge of delirium, then toppling over it with him in my mouth. I wanted to taste his come, and then taste it some more, swallow it down while he plunged back and forth, mashing his mess with my spit and saliva, till it bubbled out of my straining lips, and dripped down on to my tits. Fuck, I wanted that *so* bad.

But I also knew what the consequence would be, one more notch on the Big Man's bedpost, one more conquest to be bragged about later. 'Yeah, that Witch Bitch? You should've seen her, sucking my prick and drinking my muck, she couldn't get enough of it.' You could see the thoughts forming in his mind already. I glanced up at him, all wide-eyed and innocent, and, even though his eyes were closed tight, I just knew what was going through his head. Time, I think, for a change.

I looked over at his boys. All five of them were watching now, and a couple were jerking off. I banished that thought straight away. There's a lot of things that turn me on, but watching a guy jerk off on his own, that's right up there with the best of them. I tore my eyes away from their cocks and tried to catch their eyes. And, all the while, I was sucking and slurping, feeling the vein pulse against my hot tongue, tasting his pre-come as it started to form.

It was Butch who bit first. I knew he would. I don't know how, but I did. His mouth was wide, his cock was hard, and his eyes were popping out of his head. But I caught his gaze and I locked it down, then turned just a little, to give him a better view of the action.

I withdrew Bill's prick from my mouth with a plop, smiled, and then started licking it. Slowly, languorously, sweetly, like it was the best-tasting Popsicle I'd ever got my lips around.

Every so often I'd pop it back in, give it a suck and a bit of deep throat. Still slow, still gentle. And so inviting, like, wouldn't *you* like a taste of this meat? Wouldn't *you* like to feel it slipping in between your lips? Come on, Butchy boy, every guy gets curious once in a while, and, believe me, you're not gonna find a better cock than this. But you'd better make your mind up fast, better get your sweet little ass down here soon. You don't want Bill to finish before you can have your share, do you?

Butch's fist was pounding now. I reached my free hand out towards him, stretched and brushed the tip of his cock. He gasped and his own hand dropped away; instinctively, he shuffled forward, and I grasped him, pulled him closer, then pulled him down. Now he was crouching at my side, his face just a few inches away from mine. Away from Bill's prick.

I quit licking and whispered, 'You want a taste?'

Butch's head swivelled to stare at me, his eyes wide, his mouth still open, his tongue licking nervously at his bottom lip. Indecision, fear and, yes, desire. He wanted a taste.

I was jerking Bill hard now, to keep his mind on the job. His eyes were open now, and I could see a shadow of doubt in there, wondering what was going on. But I know how a guy's mind works. Get him worked up far enough, and close enough to coming, and it's the only thing in the whole world he cares about. And you can bend him into any shape you want to. 'Go on, Butch, do it. You'll never get another chance.'

I sucked again, flicked my tongue across the tip, boring it into the slit at the end, then pointed it straight towards Butch. 'Suck him,' I whispered, and Butch started to suck, first leaning and then almost leaping forward, and burying that stiff prick deep into his mouth.

I stepped back and buttoned my blouse. As I wiped my mouth, I heard gasps from around me and saw eyes flit to Bill's face. But Bill didn't care; he was right on the cusp now, and nothing was going to stop him. A hand wrapped itself round the back of Butch's skull, forced his face closer in, pushing that cock deeper down. I heard Butch gag, and thought for a moment that he might break away. But Bill pushed in deeper and the crisis was past. Bill was fucking his best buddy's throat, and both hands were on Butch's head now, as the come built up and his ball bag tightened and POW!

Butch was in trouble. I could hear him splutter and trying to swallow, to keep himself from choking more. But Bill wasn't letting go for anything. He was pumping hard and crying out loudly, 'Oh, God, oh, fuck, oh, don't stop now!'

His friends were standing there in absolute horror, watching the star of the football team, the frat-boy super-stud, the biggest and loudest kid in the college, slamming his spunk down another guy's throat, and loving – no, adoring – every minute of it.

Now Butch was holding him, his hands on Bill's ass, sucking the last few drops from his dick, breaking to lick it and kiss the boy's balls. And that, with the sweetest, most beautiful timing you could ever hope to encounter, was when the door to the ladies' room came flying open, and in stepped Sam with a face like thunder, and I don't know who looked the more surprised.

Bill and his mates to see him there. Or Sam, as he took in the scene spread out before him – four guys standing with their trousers down, all of them mastur-bating furiously, while the fifth was still sucking the big man's cock, come running down his scarlet chin, and dripping on to his jacket. Oh, and a girl who was pressed up against the washbasins, her eyes wide and her face all flustered, as though she really didn't want to be here, but had somehow been forced to stay and watch.

Sam swooped, and two other guys, a bartender and a bouncer, followed. Bodily, they grabbed the guys, didn't even give them a chance to pull up their pants. One under each arm, shouting and struggling, they were carried from the bathroom and deposited in the corridor, for all to see their discomfort and more. Even Bill, big Bill, with his cock all soft and sticky, was thrown out to his adoring public and, before I'd even left the room, Sam's arm solicitously round my shoulder, the word was going round.

First a whisper, then a Chinese whisper. Bill and his friends, sucking cock in the bathroom. Swallowing come and loving it all. Hey, no one here is down on gays – I once heard that ours was the most 'out' campus in America, and even the jocks tended to let them alone. But there's a big difference between being gay and being a loud-mouthed hypocrite, and Bill, I'm afraid, had crossed that line big time.

Sam held me still for a moment. 'You don't need anything? Is there anyone I should call?'

'No, really, I'm OK.' A crowd was gathering around us, all ears straining to catch every word. 'They never touched me. I was so scared, but I think they were more interested in each other.'

'Are you going to call the cops?'

Of course, he was probably more worried about his licence than me. 'No, there's no reason. They didn't do anything to me. Just … well, I hope that never happens to me again.'

Sam smiled. 'Don't you worry about that, sweetie. Not around here anyway. The lot of them are barred for life and, if anybody asks me why, I'll tell them straight. I know a lot of things go on in those bathrooms that I'm not supposed to find out about, and that's fine, just so long as they do it in private. But out in the open like that? It's disgusting, and it's insulting.' He looked up to where Bill and one of the others were still standing by the main door, their faces mute masks of shock and horror. 'You hear that?' Sam shouted. 'You want to suck each other's cocks, do it in your own homes. Not mine.'

And that was it. If anyone had still been wondering what all the fuss was about, now they knew. And I knew that, by first class tomorrow, the whole campus would have heard about it.

And that suited me just fine. I adjusted my blouse, gave my mouth one last wipe, then went to the bar and ordered a drink. Three different guys all offered to pay for it, so I let each of them buy me a refill. After everything that I'd just been through tonight, well, let's just say I was feeling mighty thirsty. And I had some unfinished business with a stiff prick to conclude.

141

Seeing in the New Year
Morwenna Drake

Gwen counted off on her fingers. Twenty-four leek tartlets, eighty canapés, two vegetarian quiches and sixty sausages on sticks. And it was only eight o'clock. 'Only salad, two hot quiches, crudités and the pear tatin to do,' Gwen muttered. 'And those desserts in the fridge. How the hell did Rebecca do all this on her own the last three years?'

Sweeping a strand of hair back from her face, Gwen fetched some double cream, pausing briefly to relish the cold air of the fridge. She'd been in the hotel kitchen since lunchtime; it was near dark now and she was exhausted, but it beat sitting at home with just a bottle of wine for company.

Gwen set about whipping the cream, glancing down at her tatin recipe and taking a gulp of red wine as she did so. Careless and distracted, she slopped wine over her handwritten recipe.

'Shit, shit, shit,' she cursed. One for the wasted wine, one for the sodden recipe and one for the hell of it. The paper tore as she hastily tried to pat it dry. Resisting another expletive, Gwen took three deep breaths before reciting her calming mantra. 'Too many cooks spoil the broth, but one in haste will screw it up completely.'

The recipe was salvageable; it just needed some Sellotape. As Gwen made her way to the stairs which led up to the hotel, she paused to glance in the mirror. If she was going to venture into the hotel proper, she ought to look respectable. Her make-up had effectively vanished in the heat of the kitchen, but she was passable. She straightened her apron then continued upstairs.

The hotel was deserted. With most of the room keys missing from behind the reception desk, Gwen guessed the owners were dealing with guests. She called out anyway. 'Ian? Marcie? I'm just grabbing the Sellotape.' Gwen leaned over the desk to pilfer the tape but, as she turned to go, a moan made her pause. 'Ian?' she called hesitantly.

The sound came again, from one of the side rooms off reception. Gwen headed tentatively towards the open door with visions of Ian lying pinned beneath a toppled ladder, yet a third moan convinced her that this was not a man in pain.

With both curiosity and apprehension, Gwen peered through the door. A man was seated on an armchair, his head back and his eyes closed. His arms and legs were spread wide. His coat was still around his shoulders, but his trousers were discarded on the floor. Kneeling between his parted thighs with her back to Gwen was a blonde woman.

For a moment, Gwen was confused as to what she was witnessing. Then the woman shifted and Gwen saw her lips clamped around the man's cock. The woman's mouth slid back up its length, leaving a ring of bright-red lipstick near the base. She teased the tip with her tongue as if it was some delightful dish she was savouring, before taking in his whole length again. The man groaned, his fingers digging into the chair. Gwen's gasp of shock drew the man's attention. He opened his eyes to stare at her blearily as the woman continued her ministrations.

'Is my room ready yet?' the man asked.

Gwen's mouth opened and closed. She couldn't stop her eyes from flicking back to the woman's bright-red lips.

'Well?' he demanded irritably. 'We've been waiting for fifteen minutes.'

Gwen thought she might faint with all the blood that rushed to her cheeks. She was rescued by the polite voice of Ian who appeared behind her. 'I'm dreadfully sorry, Mr Tighe. Your room is ready now if you'd like to come with me?'

'About time.' The man stood, dislodging the girl.

Gwen turned away quickly, and found Ian staring at her, his expression more quizzical than annoyed.

'S-Sellotape,' Gwen stammered, holding up the dispenser as proof. He nodded, a wry smile on his lips, and Gwen hurried away before her blush got any deeper.

The kitchen seemed a cool paradise in comparison. She stood, breathing hard, trying to recover herself. Her skin was on fire, and she struggled not to remember red lips wrapped around a pink phallus. She busied herself fetching and weighing ingredients, drawing composure from the familiar tasks. By the time Ian descended the stairs, she felt almost herself again.

'I hope you weren't too embarrassed up there,' he said.

'Me? Embarrassed? No. I thought Mr Tighe might have been though.'

Ian chuckled. 'Not at all, although I think he was a bit travel weary. Mr Tighe normally gains pleasure from being watched, you know. It adds piquancy.'

Gwen stared at him, trying to get her head around this novel concept. Then she narrowed her eyes suspiciously. 'Just what kind of private New Year's Eve party are you and Marcie holding here?'

Ian, an ex-rugby player with a filthy sense of humour and wandering hands, looked abashed for the first time in their acquaintance. 'We've held these parties for almost six years. It's only for particular clientele, and only on

New Year's Eve. I thought Rebecca explained all this to you yesterday when she asked you to cover her shift?'

'She said it was all a bit … specialised,' Gwen admitted, trying to recall Rebecca's exact words. 'But she gave the impression it was more sort of fancy dress and frolics.'

'There is some dressing-up,' Ian admitted. He was looking more uncomfortable by the second. 'Look, if there's a problem, we can always arrange a little extra in your pay packet and –'

'No, no, that's fine,' Gwen said hastily. He made it sound like blackmail. 'A job's a job. I'm just here to cook. What goes on upstairs doesn't concern me most nights. I don't see why tonight should be any different.'

Ian's shoulders sagged with relief. 'Thanks, Gwen. I'm sorry Rebecca didn't tell you the full story, but then she is very discreet. Speaking of which, I hate to ask this outright, but … you won't mention this to anyone, will you? Our clientele are very private.'

The anxious look was creeping across Ian's face again and Gwen was becoming increasingly nervous with his questioning. She sought desperately to lighten the mood and prove she had no issues. Seizing upon the plate of sausages in front of her, Gwen picked one up as she said, 'Absolutely not, Ian. I swear the only thing that will pass my lips about tonight will be this bit of sausage.'

Gwen popped the sausage into her mouth, trying to chew and smile at the same time. Ian stared at her, and

Gwen paled as realisation hit her like a wall of water. 'That's not … I mean, Mr Tighe … I didn't mean –' Her explanation was cut off by Ian's howl of laughter.

'Oh, Gwen! That's priceless!' Ian had tears in his eyes. Gwen sought desperately for the words to explain but Ian was already heading upstairs, chuckling to himself. At the bottom of the stairs, he paused and turned. 'I know this is a difficult time of year for you, Gwen, what with Roger leaving you a few years back and all that. But Marcie and I really appreciate you covering at such short notice, and being so discreet about it. So, when everything's done here, just feel free to head home and grab yourself something from the wine cellar as well. Call it a bonus. Or –' he paused dramatically '– you could always join us upstairs …'

Gwen's jaw was in danger of dropping open in shock. Ian gave her a bold grin before taking the stairs two at a time. Gwen shook her head, trying to dispel all the confusing thoughts crowding it.

'Cooking. That's what I do,' she declared resolutely to no one in particular. 'What goes on upstairs doesn't interest me at all.' She almost believed herself.

It was close to nine o'clock, so Gwen turned her attention back to the food and the next hour was taken up with final preparations. With only three of them on the staff rota that night, Ian and Marcie came down themselves to ferry the food up to the dining room. As Marcie was heading upstairs with two quiches, Gwen saw a flash of stocking and a diamanté garter beneath her pencil skirt.

I guess it's not just the guests enjoying themselves tonight then, she thought wryly. The idea didn't shock her as much as she thought it might. Ian and Marcie were laidback, always chatty and entertaining company, but they would often exchange secret smiles and whispers. Now Gwen had a good idea what they were whispering about.

Not wanting another grilling from either of them, Gwen carried on as if it was just a normal night. Neither of the owners mentioned anything, but Marcie did spare her a wink as she picked up the platter of sausages.

Damn it, he told her! Gwen threw a flan tin into the dishwasher with a roughness it didn't deserve. Yet, after a few moments, she began to see the funny side and was smiling to herself when she started to scrub down the table.

The back door flew open and a man stumbled in, startling Gwen. He made a curious sight, sporting a thick blue fleece on his top half and shiny black skintight trousers with a large silver zip over the crotch. Moving her eyes swiftly upwards, Gwen saw a black collar with silver studs encircling his throat. He stared at her in confusion.

'Can I help you?' she asked hesitantly.

At that moment, a woman with long blonde hair, heavy

eyeliner and deep-plum lipstick appeared behind the man. She wore a long coat, buttoned at the top but open at her waist to show flashes of red suspenders and black stockings as she walked. Shapely black boots rose to just below her knees.

'There you are, dog! What are you doing?'

The man cowered down, reaching a hand out plaintively, but the woman swatted him away with a riding crop that landed a stinging slap on his wrist. The man yelped. 'I was just looking for the entrance, my lady,' he whimpered as he cradled his hand.

'Does this look like an entrance to you? Stupid creature.' At that moment, the woman became aware of Gwen, meeting her gaze as a queen would a subject. 'I'm terribly sorry that my dog disturbed you.'

Gwen was bemused and intrigued. 'No problem. The front door is round the corner that way.'

The woman nodded, turning to leave before a thought occurred to her. 'Will there be syllabub this evening?'

'Er, yes. A lemon one, with shortbread fingers.'

The woman frowned. 'It was champagne last year. Quite delicious.' Her manner was so imperious Gwen felt some understanding as to why the man cowered at her displeasure.

'That was Rebecca cooking last year,' Gwen explained hastily. 'There's champagne jelly this year, though, with raspberries.'

The woman nodded, favouring Gwen with a small smile. 'I look forward to it. Come, dog.' She strode out, with the man following her. He returned a few seconds later to close the door he'd left open, with an apologetic bob of the head.

Gwen stood transfixed, amused and stunned in equal measure. Just what sort of party was this?

'Certainly nothing I want to get involved with,' she murmured, as she returned to scrubbing the table. Yet curiosity burned within her. Her sexual experiences with Roger had been mostly missionary and rarely varied, although ultimately he'd left her for someone younger. Was that why? Just what else was on offer that she was missing?

The rest of the night went without incident. Dishes were sent up in batches, the plates left upstairs to be collected in the morning. When the kitchen was clean, the ovens cool, and she'd seen neither Ian nor Marcie for more than an hour and a half, Gwen decided it was home time.

As she hung up her apron, she glanced at the clock: eleven-thirty. Just time to drive home, open a bottle of wine and see in the New Year in front of the TV. Yet, as she turned the lights off, she thought of Mr Tighe and his moans of pleasure seemed like a whispered echo around the dark kitchen. Gwen glanced upwards, her skin tingling, as she heard real laughter drifting down.

Should I? Ian did invite me. But he might have been joking. Still …

Even as her brain was considering the options, her feet were climbing the stairs. Her hand trembled as she pushed open the door to the hotel, but they were shivers of excitement. The empty corridor sapped her resolve a little, reminding her that she could head back without anyone knowing. Then her gaze alighted on the dining-room door where a sign declared 'Dinner is served' in an elegant flowing script.

I'll just see how the buffet looks, she thought to herself. After all that work I did, it's only fair to have a peek.

She crept across the hallway, so alert for footsteps that, when a giggle permeated the dining-room door, Gwen literally jumped. After a moment, she continued forward, grasped the door handle and twisted it slowly, anxious not to make a noise. Her heart jumped as the mechanism clicked. Hardly daring to breathe, she opened the door a crack and peered inside.

The room was lit by candelabras and low overhead lighting. The tables with food were plain enough in outline on her left and, as her eyes adjusted, Gwen recognised some of her dishes. The champagne jellies sparkled in the flickering candlelight; the chocolate fountain glistened as it flowed with syrupy slowness.

The furniture had been rearranged and, in the dim light, it took Gwen some moments to figure out what she was seeing. Armchairs and couches had been brought in from other rooms and arranged round the walls, leaving a large central space where shadows twisted and writhed. Gwen realised that over a dozen people were copulating on the floor, some in couples, others in larger groups. Her eyes widened and her heart raced as she watched.

A woman with pigtails and a lacy bra arched her back languorously as a man buried his face in her groin, lapping at the flesh beyond her curls. To their right, a man was on his knees, his skinny buttocks clenched with exertion as he hammered hard and fast into a woman on all fours. Gwen watched the man climax, his fingers digging into the woman's fleshy thighs, before her glance strayed to the woman. It was evident, even in the dimness, that she was far from her own orgasm. Breathing heavily, the man pulled himself from the woman and groped round on the floor.

He's so tiny! No wonder the poor woman isn't satisfied. Gwen couldn't prevent the thought skittering over her brain. The man ceased groping as he found a silver vibrator. Gwen felt her nipples tighten in anticipation as the man lined it up against his frustrated partner. Feeling it pressing against her, the woman moaned and swayed backwards. As the man inserted it slowly and carefully, a look of ecstasy crossed her face and her moan this time was one of pure pleasure. The man worked carefully, twisting and sliding the toy within the woman. His look of absolute concentration fascinated Gwen almost as much as the woman's blissful expression.

Gwen's blood was heated by the spectacle and the lips of her sex began to tingle. She could feel her heartbeat rippling through her loins as the woman climaxed with a great cry. As the woman slumped down, Gwen's sense told her it was time to leave before she was spotted, but instead her eyes roved over the shadows, hungry for more.

A figure on the right drew Gwen's attention as he stepped from the gloom, a man with a six-pack worthy of a magazine cover wearing a bow tie, shirt-cuffs, and nothing else. He carried a tray filled with canapés and had a crisp white towel draped over his arm.

For a moment, Gwen thought he might spot her, and a thrill of fearful excitement ran through her. Yet he turned to his right, stepping over writhing couples to lie down on the floor, stretched out full length. He carefully arranged the canapés over himself from neck to knees before lying back very still. Within moments, a crowd of hungry guests had surrounded him. Some delicately plucked the canapés from his chest with their teeth; others picked them up and fed them to partners, while some descended on him with eager mouths as if his skin was just as tasty as the morsels that adorned it.

One woman selected a large vol-au-vent filled with mushroom pâté, scooped out the contents and smeared it over his member which twitched under her fingers. Gwen felt an answering twinge of pleasure in her sex. The woman's lips closed around the waiter's shaft. As she sucked the delicacy from his skin, the waiter's eyes glazed and every muscle in his body tensed as he fought to maintain his composure. Gwen was transfixed.

The woman pulled away, leaving the man's cock erect and glistening. She selected another canapé, then set to gorging herself again in the same way. The waiter shuddered as she eagerly enjoyed two delicacies at once.

Gwen's breath was coming in tiny gasps as she watched. She had tested the vol-au-vents herself that very afternoon. She remembered the creaminess of them on her tongue, and she wondered what it tasted like when smeared on warm living skin.

As the woman's lips slid up and down his shaft, the waiter's shoulders arched as he held back a groan and a tartlet rolled from his chest on to the floor. What a waste, Gwen thought but then she jumped as she detected footsteps behind her. She leaped away from the door. With her heart hammering at the threat of discovery, she ran most of the way up the hotel stairs, and pressed back against the wall out of sight. Once she had heard the dining-room door open and close, Gwen prepared to return downstairs but a cry made her pause.

'Not good enough, dog!' Coming from the first floor, she recognised the voice of the woman from the kitchen.

Curiosity enticed her up the last few stairs, the lips of her sex so flushed with arousal that they rubbed together with each step in a way which was both excruciating and delightful.

Gwen followed the swishing sound of a riding crop to an open door. Although the woman and her companion were behind the door, Gwen could see them in the wardrobe mirror. The man knelt hunched on the floor, polishing a boot furiously. His trousers were round his ankles, his arse bared to the woman who sat behind him in a chair, her un-booted leg dangling lazily over the arm. Her coat had been discarded on the bed, and Gwen could see not just her stockings but also a fishnet bra through which her nipples peeked.

As Gwen watched, the crop flashed out towards the man's buttocks. He gave a strangled squeak but Gwen saw his cock twitch. It was fully engorged, the tip slick with his barely restrained juices.

'I want every speck of dirt gone, dog.'

As the man doubled his efforts, the woman's free hand fell to her crotch and she began to pleasure herself as she watched him. Gwen's fingers twitched at the idea and her hand slipped into her trousers, under her panties. She was surprised at the wetness she found there and shuddered with pleasure as she imitated the woman.

'You like to watch, do you?'

The voice behind Gwen made her tear her hand away

and hold it guiltily behind her back. Coming towards her was a man wearing an elegant dressing gown, one of his own presumably. He had strong legs and walked barefoot. From the way his dark hair silvered at the temples, Gwen guessed he was a similar age to her. His eyes were deep brown and serious, but they were tempered by a wicked smile.

'In that case,' he added, stopping before her, 'I have just the room for you.'

'No, you don't understand. I'm the chef,' Gwen said hastily.

He raised an eyebrow as if in disbelief, but added, 'But how fortunate! I was going to ask Ian to pass on my compliments. The tatin was delicious. What was it that flavoured the cream?'

'Cinnamon.' Focusing on a safe, familiar topic relaxed Gwen somewhat. When he offered her his champagne, she readily accepted. She had meant to take only a sip, but her mouth was so dry she emptied the glass. The man smiled approvingly. She handed back the glass, saying, 'Thank you, but I must be going.'

'Really? Don't you want to see this room? My name's Robert, by the way.'

'Gwen.'

'Delightful. Do you live nearby, Gwen?'

The comfortable small talk distracted Gwen as Robert guided her down the hall to the last door on the right.

She recognised it as the conference room, but inside it was transformed. Virtually every mirror from the hotel had been placed within to reflect a hundred times over the people pleasuring each other.

'Shall we?' Robert asked casually.

No, we shouldn't. I should go home. There's a bottle of wine in the fridge and I need to feed the cat. Yet Gwen's throat was too tight to speak the words and so she found herself being led across the darkened room to the far wall where the shadows were deepest and the couples fewest. Robert guided her back against the wall and began to undress her. Gwen was unresisting, hypnotised by the tableau surrounding her.

Two men were spooning on the floor, moaning and whispering together. Next to them a woman sat astride a man, her breasts bouncing as she rode him furiously. Another woman was lying sandwiched between two men, both driving into her with slow deliberate strokes.

'Much more suitably attired,' Robert murmured as he discarded the last of Gwen's clothes. He removed his own gown to match her nakedness and a surge of heat ran through Gwen to see his erection reaching towards her. Then Robert was on his knees, kissing her thighs. The touch of his lips drove all other thoughts from Gwen's mind. As Robert's tongue sought out her hidden flesh, she had to steady herself against the wall, moaning softly. In a matter of moments, Robert's experienced tongue coaxed an orgasm from her so explosive Gwen thought she might faint with the pleasure.

'I'm guessing you needed that,' Robert commented with a smile as he stood up.

Gwen had no voice to reply and no will to resist when he guided her to a nearby table. He gently bent her forward over it, then spread her legs wide. He stood behind her and she felt the tip of his shaft press against her slit. He paused, allowing her to savour the anticipation, then slid inside her. Gwen gave something between a laugh and a gasp as Robert's cock parted her sensitive flesh.

His stamina was amazing. It felt like he thrust into her for hours on end, and all the time Gwen's eyes remained open, mesmerised by the surrounding couples. She came again before he reached his own climax. When he was spent, he leaned over to whisper in her ear. He described in such delicious detail the exploits of those around them that Gwen almost felt as if she shared each couple's pleasure herself. When he hardened within her again, she was ready for him.

Sated by two orgasms already, Gwen held out longer this time. Robert went slowly and gently until he could hold back no more. Gwen urged him on until his spasm of pleasure rocketed her into her own orgasm. Both of them were panting by the time they finished. Lost in a haze of pleasure, Gwen jumped when the ornate clock on the wall struck twelve.

'Happy New Year, Gwen,' Robert whispered breathlessly in her ear.

'Indeed, it is,' she replied with a smile.

Show-offs
Heather Towne

Lora was lying next to me on the blanket, staring up at the clouds. The warm sun bathed us, the burbling creek further soothing our cares away. 'Great idea to have a picnic today,' I said to my wife, nestling my head more comfortably in my clasped hands.

'Mmmm,' she murmured. 'Even better than watching football?'

I looked at her. She was wearing a blue crop-top and tight black shorts, and her hands were folded across her bare stomach, breasts rising and falling, long tanned legs stretched out shining in the sun. Her pretty face was relaxed, dreamy – like her body – thick red hair cushioning her head.

'Well, almost,' I responded, rolling over on to my side

and sliding a hand on to her stomach, and rubbing.

'Hey, now,' she breathed, 'what are you up to?'

'About seven inches,' I replied, gliding my fingers up the smooth bronze skin of her stomach so that they nudged the bottom of her filled-out top. I circled them around the mounded outline of a breast and gently squeezed.

'Hey!' Lora exclaimed, turning her head and staring at me. 'Just what *do* you think you're doing?'

'Having some dessert?' I suggested, squeezing her breast more warmly. I moved my head over and pressed my lips against the pointed indentation of her nipple.

Lora moaned, and I quickly wormed my hand right under her top and grasped the hot firm flesh of her breast, sucking on her stiffened nipple through the thin cotton.

Until I heard laughter, and jerked my head up. Two men were setting up their fishing gear about a hundred yards farther down the creek bank. They weren't laughing at Lora and me, though, they hadn't noticed us yet, but they were clearly in viewing range. As was the couple now hiking along the trail over on the other side of the creek, off to our left.

I rolled over on to my back again. 'I guess I'll have to have that dessert at home,' I said sheepishly.

But I'd aroused something in my wife more than just her nipple. The tawny redhead was usually too modest to even kiss in public, but the warm sun and the cool wine had apparently gone to her head, because she reached over and grasped my cock through my jeans, enveloping the erection in her warm soft hand and squeezing.

I jumped.

'You can't stop what you started now,' she purred, openly caressing my hard-on.

I stared at her, and she rolled over on to her side and kissed me. Her red lips were wet and tangy, her blue eyes sparkling. I groaned, revelling in the twin heat of the sun and my wife's rubbing hand.

She kissed one of my nipples through my white T-shirt. Her agile tongue flicked at it, swirled around it, sending wicked tingling sensations shooting down to my cock. She had a firm grip on my swollen shaft now, pumping.

The men's laughter carried over on the warm breeze, and I clearly heard the twin plops of their fishing lures being cast into the water. Looking past Lora's head, I could see the couple across the creek stopping to examine something they'd picked up on the trail. And then I looked into Lora's eyes, feeling her stroking hand and sucking mouth all through me, and I didn't give a damn about any of them any more. If little Miss Modesty didn't, why should I?

I reached over with my left hand and planted it in between my wife's legs, giving tit for tat, this for that. Two could play at the erotic public petting game, all the better.

Lora moaned, her eyelashes fluttering, as I cupped her sex through her shorts, squeezing the springy mound. I could feel the heat, the wetness, the fur of her pussy right through the thin material of her shorts and panties. Her hand hugging and rubbing my cock urged me on.

I caressed her pussy, moving my hand up and down, fondling her most intimate area with fingers and fingertips. Her tits heaved on her chest, her own fingers clutching, choking, chuffing my cock. She pushed her mound up against my hand and I pressed hard and deep, Lora doing the same on my outthrust organ.

We rubbed together, stroking faster and faster. She gasped, shuddered, and I knew that I'd found her clit, the sensitive little sex button swollen up so hard I could feel it through the cloth. I buffed it with my fingertips, Lora jacking me with the same wicked intent.

We were both close to coming, glaring into each other's glassy eyes, petting heavier and hornier than we'd ever done, even when we'd been dating. The open air and our own open exhibition had sent our senses soaring.

I grabbed the turned-on babe in my arms and pulled her over on top of me, kissing her on the mouth. I needed to feel all of her against me, the pair of us rubbing full-length together.

Her curvy body melded to mine, her clothed pussy now covering my jeaned cock, her lips moving passionately against mine. I plunged my hands into the back of her shorts and under her panties and grabbed on to her bare butt cheeks, kneading the taut mounds.

Exposure

She moaned into my mouth, undulating against my cock. I shot my tongue into her mouth and tangled it with her tongue, as she ran her fingers through my hair. We frenched and fondled one another – out there under the sun on that exposed creek bank.

Lora captured my thrashing tongue between her teeth and sucked on it, bobbing her head up and down. I moaned, kneading the heated flesh of her buttocks and pumping my cock against her pussy, the length of steel pulsating to the pounding beat of my heart.

The wind rustled the leaves in the trees and something splashed in the water, but we weren't paying any attention to nature, or nature-lovers. Lora was riding my cock and sucking on my tongue, as I groped her butt cheeks and frotted her pussy.

Suddenly, she gasped, and shuddered, biting into my tongue. I grunted, coming too, the erotic friction and the wanton heat of my wife making me cream my pants over and over.

An eternity later, Lora rolled off of me. We lay on our backs, panting.

The kids and the couple watched us, as we self-consciously gathered up our picnic stuff and walked, stiff-legged, up the bank and through the trees to our car.

* * *

I thought that would be our one and only furtive foray into public sex. But, to my amazement, it proved to be just a dry-run.

Our sex life had been satisfying up to that point, before and after marriage. We'd tried a few kinks, experimenting, attempting to add some additional spice to our love-making. Role-playing and mild bondage, for example. But, after that first taboo experience, Lora took exhibitionism and ran with it, dragging me willingly along for the ride, our sex life rocketing from traditional to torrid.

The second session came out of the blue two days later, the spontaneity and danger of it heightening the erotic sensations. We were out for a walk, when all of a sudden some dark clouds rolled in and it started raining. We got soaked, running for the partial cover of a church doorway.

And as we huddled together in the arched entranceway, in front of the huge oaken door with the cross on it, Lora kissed me. Then she grabbed me in her arms and *really* kissed me. I kissed back, heavily, heatedly, smothering her mouth with mine.

Our sodden discomfort was forgotten, as I kissed Lora's chin, her neck. She moaned and tilted her head back, and I ran my tongue up and down the silky skin of her neck. Then we met at the mouth again, consuming one another.

It had turned cool with the rain, but that didn't matter.

We were burning with our own special kind of heat. Lora pulled my T-shirt right up to my chin, exposing my glistening chest. She ran her damp hands all over my bare skin, her fingers latching on to my nipples and pinching, before cupping my pecs and teasing a tingling nipple with her tongue.

'Fuck!' I groaned, tilting my head back.

Lora quickly rained kisses down on my neck, then bit into my Adam's apple.

I tore her light jacket away, baring her chest to the elements in her green halter top. The rain soaked in, highlighting the plush curves of her breasts, the pointed excitement of her nipples. I gripped her tits through her top and squeezed the lovely pair. Then bent my head down and sucked an engorged nipple into my mouth, pulling on it through the wet cotton.

'Yes! They're watching us! There are people watching us!' Lora exulted, digging her fingernails into my scalp.

I'd forgotten where we were, and suddenly became self-conscious. I'd been an altar boy at one time, after all. I tried to pull my head back, but Lora held on tight, keeping me pinned to her chest.

There was nothing to do but what I'd been doing. And I did it joyously, sucking on Lora's jutting nipples, mouth full of damp cloth and rubbery bud, wet and wild. I pushed her tits together and slashed my tongue across both rigid tips at once, Lora shivering in my hands.

There were all kinds of people out on the sidewalks and in cars on the street, staring at us as they rushed by in the rain, watching me urgently suck on my wife's nipples. They saw clearly, if briefly, exactly what we were up to. And all the attention added fuel to our raging sexual fire.

Lora let go of my head and dove her hands down on to my cock, clutching the pulsing appendage like she'd done down by the creek. Only this time she wanted the feel of the real thing, and was determined to get it. She pushed me back from her chest and gripped my belt with one hand and my fly with the other, then unzipped me. She dug around in my pants and shorts and pulled my hard-on out into the open.

The rain splashed against the sensitive skin, making me jerk. Lora let it get wet, cradling my throbbing erection, before stroking it, swirling her hand up and down the veiny length.

A pedestrian gasped, another cheered, a couple of cars honked. I just moaned my appreciation, luxuriating in the hot tug of Lora's hand on my shaft. I leaned back against the doorway, all-cock now, my wife pulling me longer and harder, cupping my balls and squeezing.

I thought she was going to jack me off right then and there. But she had another, better idea.

She let go of my dick, leaving me straining upwards, pink and exposed. She unbuttoned her jeans and slid them and her panties down to her knees, exposing her pussy. Then she waited, leaning back all sultry against the doorway, thighs glistening, ginger fur of her pussy winking with moisture.

I stepped forward and covered her bared sex with my hand. She moaned, tits shivering. I pushed up her top, fully exposing her breasts. They shone with moisture, like her pussy. I clutched a lush tit with my left hand, petting her cunt with my right.

'Yes! Yes!' Lora shrieked, over the rumbling thunder, the hiss of the rain streaming down. For all to hear and see.

I pressed two fingertips through the silken folds of her pussy lips and sank them inside, shot the pair of digits deep into her, all the way up to the third knuckle. She spasmed, her pussy muscles clamping down on my buried digits. I pumped, finger-fucking my wife, feeling up her tits.

She clutched at the doorway, writhing against the door. I moved closer, pumped faster. I squeezed her tits so hard the flesh burned red under my hand, her stiffened, shiny nipples almost popping right off, as I recklessly plunged her pussy with my fingers.

There was no mistaking what we were doing, my cock jutting out and jumping like a pink obscenity, my fingers plugged into Lora's pussy, her semi-nude body blazing golden brown in the falling silver rain. It was an exhibition of utter eroticism and abandon, for anyone to stop and gawk at if they didn't mind getting wet. Like my pistoning fingers.

Lora suddenly grasped the wrist of my loving hand. Her eyes were lit up like I'd never seen them before, wild with lust. 'Fuck me!' she hissed. 'With your cock!'

I pulled my hand off her tit, my fingers out of her slit, and stood back, hesitating.

Somebody yelled, 'Go for it, man!' And I did.

I got a grip on my cock and pushed the mushroomed head into Lora's fur. She groaned, as I found her inner wetness with my dick, parting her pussy lips with my hood.

I went in slowly, so all the gawping spectators could see, inch by bloated inch sliding inside the hot, tight, beautiful lady, until my balls cushioned up against her fur, and I was buried in her cunt.

Thunder rolled and lightning flashed across the sky, as the rain poured down. I clamped on to Lora's tits and pumped my hips, fucking her. She grasped my clenching butt cheeks and wildly kissed me, frenched me, my cock ploughing back and forth in her pussy.

It was outrageous and amazing – fucking my wife in that church doorway in the middle of a rainstorm at the height of rush hour – and utterly, fantastically erotic. I pumped faster, harder, Lora's body jerking with my every maddened thrust, her tits jumping in my hands.

'Oh, God, yes! Fuck me! Fuck me!' she cried, loud enough for anyone to hear.

That did it. I spasmed, and sprayed. She screamed, shuddering with her own orgasm. I pounded into her in a frenzy, pouring out my searing lust to meet the heated gushing waves of her ecstasy.

* * *

That weekend, Lora and I attended the out-of-town wedding of one of her friends from college. I didn't care much for the friend, and the wedding dragged on forever, bringing me down with it. Afterwards, though, the ride up in the hotel elevator set my spirits soaring again.

The hotel was a towering steel and glass affair located smack in the middle of about 32 lanes of traffic, but it compensated for the terrible outside view with a pleasant indoor one. The elevator was made entirely of glass, and it looked out on to the plant-festooned, water-fountained inner courtyard of the hotel and the sheer glass face of the rooms opposite, as it ran up its track.

Lora and I were the only ones inside, and the view went from sublime to spectacular, when she suddenly stopped the car between the tenth and eleventh floors and slid the straps of her gown off her shoulders. The puffy blue dress tumbled down to her waist, revealing her full tits and ever-hard nipples.

'R-right here?' I gulped.

She nodded, walking closer.

The elevator was lit up, as were many of the rooms across the way, and there were plenty of people still milling about in the courtyard below. Everything was crystal-clear, including what I had to do. I stripped off my jacket, tie and shirt and met Lora halfway, embracing and kissing her.

Her bare breasts burned against my bare chest. Our tongues sought and found one another, entwining, our hands exploring every inch of our backs.

When we finally came up for air, we saw some people staring at us from their rooms, more looking up from the courtyard. They were obviously anxious to see some of the passion the wedding and reception had so sadly lacked, and we were only too anxious to please.

I cupped Lora's tits and swirled my tongue around her nipples, painting her pebbled areolae. She responded with a pleasured moan, and a quick unzip of her dress which left it crumpled on the floor of the elevator.

The brazen babe was now naked in my hands (and in the eyes of many), except for her sheer white stockings and shiny blue high heels. I took a moment to appreciate her glowing beauty, before making ardent love to her breasts again. I engulfed half of one of her tits with my mouth and pulled on it, then devoured and chewed on her other tit. She gripped my shoulders, gazing out at the people watching, her eyes gone misty.

171

I fed on her supple breasts, gorged on her hardened nipples, until she urgently tugged at my belt. Then I pulled back and unfastened the belt, pushed my dress pants and my shorts down and stepped out of them, my erection bobbing out and up. Lora caught my cock in her hand, making me jump. She went down on her knees and sucked the bulbous tip of my prick, making me gasp.

Looking up at me with her glittering blue eyes, my wife took more and more of my cock into her mouth, her glossy red lips widening, sliding, consuming. She swallowed up two-thirds of my pulsing member in the wet hot cauldron of her mouth. I buckled, clutching at her done-up hair, shimmering all over with a fiery heat.

Lora moved her head back and forth, sucking on my cock. I stared down at her, at the people staring up at us. Her lips glided along the glistening length of my prick, her tongue cushioning, cheeks billowing. She'd been reluctant to give me the pleasure of a blowjob in the privacy of our own bedroom in the past, but not here, out in public. She was a show-woman, her oral talents on display for all to see, and her lucky husband to fully appreciate.

She sucked hard and swift, slow and sensual, stretching me just about beyond the point of endurance. Then she pulled all the way back, letting me dangle in front of the gaping crowd, a shining snake yearning for the kiss of its mistress' lips, the hot caress of her tongue and mouth. 'Eat me,' she breathed all over my cock.

172

She rose up, and I went down. I placed my shaking hands on her shimmering thighs, rubbed up and down with my damp palms, caressing the shapely lengths of her silk-clad legs. Her pussy glistened in front of me, ginger fur twinkling with moisture.

I briefly glanced out at the people across the way, down below, then looked back into my wife's pussy. I licked my lips and took a deep breath, then plunged my face up against Lora's cunt, burying my nose in her most intimate warmth and wetness.

'Oh, God! Yes!' she cried, grabbing hold of my head.

I revelled, wallowed in her lush heated dampness, really rubbing my face in her, breathing in her spicy sweet sex scent. Then I pulled my head back a bit, so all could see. I slid my tongue out of my mouth and into the curly red pubes of Lora's pussy.

Her painted fingernails bit into my scalp, as the tip of my tongue touched the edges of her lips. Then she moaned, bowed, as I burrowed my tongue deeper, gliding through her flaps and right inside her, spearing into the velvety depths of her tunnel. I hardened my tongue inside her and moved my head back and forth, fucking the beautiful lady with my mouth.

'Oh, honey! They're all watching! They're watching you eat me!'

I rolled my eyes upwards. Lora was gazing out of the glass walls of the elevator, her wild eyes scanning the crowd up and down and across, tugging on my head with her grasping hands, undulating her sex in my face. I gripped her quivering thighs harder and pumped faster, drilling deep as I could go, fucking the vibrating woman with my tongue. The heat was intense, the moisture incredible; she was molten in my mouth.

I pulled my tongue out of her slit, and licked her pussy – long and hard and slow, up from deep in between her legs to the crowning clit of her cunt. She jerked her head down, staring at me. I grinned at her, eagerly lapping her pussy, licking up and down over and over and over.

She shook out of control under my oral onslaught. I slid my hands around her thighs and on to her buttocks, grasping the taut trembling mounds, painting her pussy with my tongue, until, after one long last loving stroke, I found her swollen clit with my lips, sealed them over her button and sucked.

'Oh, no! Yes!'

I pressed her into my mouth with my hands on her bum, my cheeks billowing, lips vaccing, sucking hard and tight on her puffed-up trigger. It was the first time I'd ever done such a thing, and here I was doing it for the first time in a transparent elevator capsule with a crowd of strangers and, perhaps, friends gathered to watch.

It was glorious, delicious, erotic and exciting as hell, sucking my wife's button in plain sight. The smell, the taste, the squirt of her hot pre-come against my chin, the passionate throb of her clit in my mouth. She had to shove me back hard before she came all over my ecstatic face.

She wanted us to come at the same time, together, really put on a show of our mutual lust and love for the crowd of onlookers. She turned around and placed her hands against one glass wall of the elevator. She bent forward at the waist, parting her long legs, pushing her cute little bubble-butt out and wagging it at me.

This was red-flag-to-a-bull stuff for me. I jumped to my feet and gripped my slippery cock and charged forward. I speared into her slit, driving deep and true into her sodden pussy.

'Yes! Fuck me!' Lora cried.

I grasped her hips and pumped mine, fucking the woman right there in that glass observation elevator. We were nude and lewd and totally on display, showing off our awesome passion.

The crowd in the courtyard had grown, people rushing in from all corners like there was a jumper on the roof, gazing up at us with open mouths and widened eyes. Couples and singles watched from the comfort of their hotel rooms, some of them fondling and nuzzling, some jacking, inspired by our erotic audacity.

I slammed back and forth inside Lora, her butt cheeks rippling with every jolt, her splayed hands squeaking on the looking-glass. She excitedly pushed back at me, and we hit the perfect rhythm; plunging deep, pulling almost all the way out, her pussy walls and lips sucking on my pistoning cock.

I burned with a glowing heat, muscles tightening all over my body and buttocks, fucking that gorgeous lady flat-out in front of an enthralled public. She pulled a hand off the glass and clutched at a tit, rolling and pulling on her nipple, getting rocked back and forth by me, her loving husband.

Suddenly, she screamed out her joy, overcome by a wicked orgasm. I watched her dance on the end of my thrusting cock, before I too exploded with orgasm, jetting inside her.

There was a spontaneous burst of applause, when Lora finally hit the button that got the elevator moving again, and we gathered up our clothes.

Our summer vacation starts next weekend. We're taking a train out to the coast and then a plane over to Europe. I can only imagine the eye-opening possibilities.

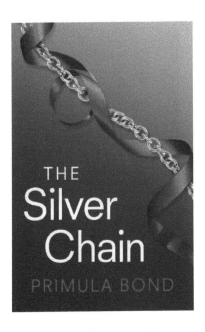

THE SILVER CHAIN – PRIMULA BOND

Good things come to those who wait…

After a chance meeting one evening, mysterious entrepreneur Gustav Levi and photographer Serena Folkes agree to a very special contract.

Gustav will launch Serena's photographic career at his gallery, but only if Serena agrees to become his companion.

To mark their agreement, Gustav gives Serena a bracelet and silver chain which binds them physically and symbolically. A sign that Serena is under Gustav's power.

As their passionate relationship intensifies, the silver chain pulls them closer together. But will Gustav's past tear them apart?

A passionate, unforgettable erotic romance for fans of *50 Shades of Grey* and Sylvia Day's *Crossfire Trilogy*.

POWER PLAY – CHARLOTTE STEIN

Now she's the boss, everything that once seemed forbidden is possible…

Meet Eleanor Harding, a woman who loves to be in control and who puts Anastasia Steele in the shade.

When Eleanor is promoted, she loses two very important things: the heated relationship she had with her boss, and control over her own desires.

She finds herself suddenly craving something very different – and office junior, Ben, seems like just the sort of man to fulfil her needs. He's willing to show her all of the things she's been missing – namely, what it's like to be the one in charge.

Now all Eleanor has to do is decide…is Ben calling the kinky shots, or is she?

Find out more at www.mischiefbooks.com

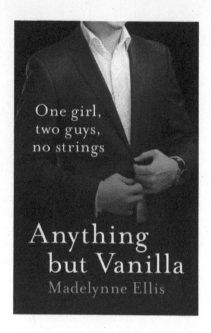

www.ingramcontent.com/pod-product-compliance
Ingram Content Group UK Ltd.
Pitfield, Milton Keynes, MK11 3LW, UK
UKHW022245180325
456436UK00001B/23